# HOW LAMAR'S BAD PRANK WON A BUBBA-SIZED TROPHY

*Crystal Allen*

Balzer + Bray
*An Imprint of HarperCollinsPublishers*

Balzer + Bray is an imprint of HarperCollins Publishers.

How Lamar's Bad Prank Won a Bubba-Sized Trophy

Library of Congress Cataloging-in-Publication Data
Allen, Crystal.
    How Lamar's bad prank won a Bubba-sized trophy / Crystal
Allen. — 1st ed.
       p.    cm.
    Summary: When thirteen-year-old, bowling-obsessed Lamar
Washington finds out that his idol is coming to town, he gets into
trouble as he tries to change his image to impress people.
    ISBN 978-0-06-199272-8 (trade bdg.)
    [1. Bowling—Fiction.  2. Conduct of life—Fiction.  3. African
Americans—Fiction.]  I. Title.
PZ7.A42527Ho  2011                        2010008229
[Fic]—dc22                                  CIP
                                              AC

Typography by Jennifer Rozbruch
11 12 13 14 15  CG/RRDB  10 9 8 7 6 5 4 3 2 1
❖

First Edition

For Reggie, Phillip, and Joshua,
the maddest, baddest, most
spectacular guys ever

## Chapter One

Since Saturday, I've fried Sergio like catfish, smashed him like potatoes, and creamed his corn in ten straight games of bowling. And it's just the middle of the week. People call Wednesday "hump day," but for Sergio it's "kicked-in-the-rump day." I'm his daddy now, the maddest, baddest, most spectacular bowler ever.

Sergio hates to lose. He's always got some lame excuse for biting the dust. Now I'm on the phone, listening to him bump his gums about how he's going to beat me tomorrow. I've heard enough, so I break him off a dose of reality.

"You couldn't outbowl me if there were two of you and I had the flu."

Sergio whines worse than a busted violin. "What do you expect? Look how long you've been bowling!"

I pretend to cry. "Hold on, let me get a tissue so I can wipe the Sergio sap leaking from my eyes. If you'd bowled with me for three years instead of playing Little League football, you'd *be* as good as I am at rolling the rock. Maybe I need better competition."

"I can beat you, Lamar. Better competition? You're just scared to face me again."

I pull the phone away and stare at it in disbelief before pressing it back to my ear. "Scared to face you? First, if I *had* your face, I'd sue my parents."

Sergio chuckles but immediately comes back. "Really? Well, sue this. You're going down. Eleven is my lucky number."

"You're going to need lucky numbers, tarot cards, rabbits' feet, four-leaf clovers—every good-luck charm you can find to beat me."

Sergio's my boy. We've been tighter than the lid on a new jar of pickles since second grade. He's good at a bunch of stuff, especially math, and he's *really* good at attracting girls. But when Sergio says *bowl*, he might as well grab one out of the kitchen cabinet and fill it with cereal.

"I'm serious, Lamar. Your streak dies at ten."

I take a deep breath and let it out so Sergio can hear it. "Let's just turn the page on this conversation and talk about something you *might* be good at. What's going on with you and Tasha? Have you mixed spit yet?"

"Timing is everything with Tasha. She's classy and I need to take it slow."

A big glob of laugh-out-loud threatens to explode in my throat. "Why don't you just say, 'No, I haven't handled my business yet'?"

Sergio's frustration speaks up. "I just can't find the right time to kiss her."

I fall across my bed laughing. "Are you serious? You and Tasha haven't done the Latin lip lock, the Tijuana tongue tango? I thought you Spanish dudes had it going on. What are you, scared? Just do it."

I knew that would get him. Sergio guards his reputation as if one day it's going to get inducted into the Smithsonian Institution.

"At least I've got a girlfriend," he says. "Anyway it's not about Tasha; it's about my birthday in six days. That's what's up. I wonder what my parents bought me."

There's no way I'm letting him off that easy. I dog him again. "If Tasha were my girl, I'd put these luscious lips of love on her every day."

Sergio fakes a sneeze. "Oh excuse me, I'm allergic to bull. See you tomorrow."

"All right," I say. "Be there at noon and don't forget to grab us a lane. Get some sleep. Maybe Tasha will visit you in your dreams wearing a sexy Mexican dress. Oh, and maybe she'll do that tap dance and snap her fingers with a long-stemmed red rose in her mouth and—"

"Shut up, Lamar. And get *my* girl out of *your* head."

"Yeah, I guess I did get carried away there. My bad. Later, Sergio."

I'm spacing out at the ceiling, wishing I had Sergio's problem. I've asked eight girls to be mine, but they all thought I was joking or had some prank waiting on 'em. Maybe I did take things a bit too far a few weeks ago when I asked four different girls to be mine on the same day. I figured one would say yes. Nobody told me girls talk to each other about stuff like that. When the final bell rang, I found out they *do* talk, and boy, it got ugly.

All four of 'em corralled me at my locker, put my business on blast, told God and everybody about how my rap is sap and my game is lame. That's when I parted my lips and said the worst thing ever.

"You took me seriously? I was just kidding around."

I waited a whole week to let things blow over before trying again. And for my own safety, I asked one girl at a time. But it didn't matter. The word was out. *He's not serious.*

They're wrong. I'm ready to hook up with somebody, and that's no joke. And when I find her, I'll handle my business, put these luscious lips of love on her—and she'll know she just got hooked up to the L-Train.

I'm up early Thursday morning. My older brother and I take turns cleaning the bathrooms, vacuuming, bustin' suds, and taking out the trash. Dad won't let us leave the house until we're done, and I'm not about to let some chump chores stop me from bowling.

All I want to do is hang out at Striker's Bowling Paradise. On the first day of summer I took my report card to Striker's and showed the manager I'd gotten the job done. In return, he gave me the only thing I wanted from him: a bowling pass.

I get two free games every day, plus rental shoes, thanks to my grades. It's a sweet deal and worth the extra effort in school. At Striker's, I dance to hip-hop, girl watch, get my bowl on, and eat all in one place. My bowling skills are ridiculous, and I prove it to anyone who wants to challenge me. On the street, I'm just Lamar, but on the lanes, they call me the King of Striker's.

Even though I'm an awesome bowler, Sergio tries to chump me about being thirteen years old and still girlfriendless. Every day I stare in the mirror, groom my fro, and proclaim today as the end of my dry spell. I point my comb at the mirror.

"You're a superfine, hot-blooded power line, and today, one lucky girl will win the Lamar lottery. Now go find your winner!"

A hard finger snap, a quick wink, and a finger point at my reflection put the finishing touches on a closed deal. I shove my comb into my back pocket, close my eyes, and clear my head.

I hate this part of my morning, but I have to do it, so I take a deep breath in through my nose. I hold that air for ten seconds before releasing it out through my mouth. I fill my lungs with big air again, hold it, and release it slowly. After ten inhales and exhales, I reach to hit the light switch and notice my fake black spider chillin' behind the soap dish. I snatch it up and shove it in my pocket. Maybe I'll find a sucker at Striker's.

In the living room, Dad's reorganizing my brother's basketball trophies on the fireplace mantel. He's usually asleep by now, because he's the night-shift security guard at the hospital.

"Hey, Dad, have you been asleep yet?"

Dad yawns. "No, not yet. Xavier got another

trophy last night: Basketball Star of the Future. I'm glad he chose to play in the YMCA league this summer. It's sure sharpened his skills."

My brother has six trophies on the mantel. Each one has a miniature gold guy at the top, posing like a real basketball stud.

I just want to snap off their tiny, shiny heads.

Right now, all I have on the mantel is promised space, but it's untouchable. Mom taped a yellow Post-it above the fireplace for all the world to read:

> This spot reserved for
> Lamar's first trophy.
> You'll always be my little
> superstar.
> Love,
> Mom

I'll never forget how Xavier blew a fuse when he read it. He stood on the other side of Mom, cut his eyes to me, and squeezed his basketball between his huge hands.

"Superstar? Everybody knows who the *real* superstar is in this family."

I shot back, "Then how's it feel being the family chump?"

Xavier went dead-red angry, and by the twisted frown on his face, he was ready to fight. When he shoved his basketball between his elbow and his armpit, I moved closer to Mom. She extended her arms to keep us apart.

With outstretched hands, she gently pulled us toward her by our shirtsleeves. With one arm around Xavier and the other around me, she held us close. Xavier's basketball fell to the floor. I exhaled. Something about her touch always calmed us. And then, in a loving voice, she killed us with kindness.

"How lucky am I? I've got two superstar sons. And best of all, they show love to their mother by showing love to each other. It just doesn't get any better than that."

Xavier broke away first, picked up his basketball, then nodded at me.

"Let's just man up and move on."

I nodded back. "Fine."

Mom was magic in motion. Just straight-up cool like that. Whether it was hugs or a quick, off-the-chain delicious meal, she knew how to shut us up and make us love each other whether we wanted to or not.

She didn't tell us she was sick until it became

obvious. Her hair fell out, she wouldn't eat, and sometimes she was so weak, Dad had to carry her from the couch to the bed.

Mom died of cancer last year, but that Post-it still hangs on. It's my piece of her, and that space is totally, hands-down, no-questions-asked, off-limits to Xavier, and he knows it.

I grab the doorknob and face Dad. "I finished my chores. I'm going to Striker's."

"Have fun."

"Do you need me to do anything before I go?"

"Nope." He blows something off the wood at the bottom of X's newest trophy.

The door whines when I open it, and Dad spins around. He rubs his eyes again.

"Did you do your breathing exercises?"

"Yes, sir. And before you ask, I have my inhaler with me."

"Good. Do you think the trophies look better this way, or . . . this way?"

"Dad, I mean, they're just stupid trophies."

His back stiffens. "Do you know what they represent?"

Yeah, a guy so stupid his brain would fit in a teaspoon. But I say what Dad expects.

"No, sir, I don't know."

"They represent achievements and possibilities. Your brother could get a full scholarship to Indiana University or Purdue, or some other really good college."

I want to warn Dad not to hold his breath, because Xavier's grades are below sea level. He'll be lucky to get a scholarship anywhere besides Punk 'n' Chump University. But Dad seems wide-awake now that we're talking about scholarships. I decide to get in the game.

"Do colleges give out bowling scholarships?"

Dad stares at the ceiling like the answer's written up there.

"I don't know. They didn't have them when I was in school. We need to check that out. As good as you are at bowling, you'd get a full ride somewhere."

As if on cue, X strolls in with an algebra book in one hand and his basketball under the other arm. He ducks his head to avoid the archway leading from the hall. School has always been year-round for X because he's forever sitting in a summer class. His first session is algebra. The second one will be algebra again because he won't pass the first session.

Xavier's seventeen, and in August, when school starts, he'll be a senior. If he bombs algebra this summer, he could also sink his chance of playing college ball.

He bumps me on his way to the kitchen. "I

know you didn't ask about bowling scholarships. Get real. Basketball and football, baby. That's a straight ticket to the NCAA."

X looks at Mom's Post-it and pushes my head. "Thought you knew that, superstar."

Dad interrupts, "Okay, that's enough. Xavier, keep your hands off your brother. And stop the sarcasm about your mother's note. How would she feel about your smart mouth?"

All three of us glance up at the mantel. Dad stands between us, but he doesn't pull us close like Mom did. He just clears his throat.

"X, get to class. Lamar, don't be out too late."

Xavier and I turn in different directions but respond the same way.

"Yes, sir."

Everybody calls Xavier "X." Sometimes they call him "Xavier the Basketball Savior," a name Dad came up with. I call him X because to me he's a mistake for which my parents owe me a long overdue "Our bad, Lamar."

I turn the doorknob and burn off. That scholarship conversation circles my brain. Who are these people who decide which sports are the good ones? I bet none of them are bowlers.

And it doesn't help much that bowling isn't big here in Coffin, Indiana. We've never hosted a professional bowling tournament or even had a pro bowler visit our lanes. We just don't get many out-of-towners here. From the interstate, people take the Coffin exit because they need gas or directions, or because they're jerks who think we've got some Guinness book graveyard on display.

Our town is named after Levi Coffin, the Underground Railroad conductor from Indiana. My teachers say he helped more than two thousand slaves to freedom. What makes that really cool is that Levi Coffin was a white dude. To me, that took guts. He deserves megaprops for what he did, and I let people know when they laugh at our town's name. They don't laugh long.

This obsession with basketball isn't just a Coffin thing. It's statewide. You can't live *or* die in Indiana without some kind of hoops connection. Newborns leave the hospital and dead folk leave this world dressed in Hoosier basketball gear.

That's why a lousy YMCA game in Coffin can end up with a standing-room-only crowd. I bet somebody older than sausage started this basketball madness. I'm going to end it. As King of Striker's, it's my job to announce that hoops has fouled out and bowling is now the maddest, baddest, most spectacular game in town.

## Chapter Two

Since Mom died, every woman in Coffin's been trying to raise me. They put me on blast, asking embarrassing questions in front of God and everybody. I'm strutting down the street when Mrs. Ledbetter waves from the side of her driveway, where she's planting flowers. She's a big woman with a butt so wide, it wipes all the dirt off the side of her car when she stands to greet me.

"Hi Lamar. Aren't you hot? You've got to be burning up with that enormous crop of hair on your scalp. You're making me hot just looking at you."

"No, ma'am. I'm not hot."

"Even though my husband's a retired barber, he still sees well enough to give you a haircut."

"I like my hair, Mrs. Ledbetter. But when I'm ready for a haircut, I'll come see Mr. Ledbetter, okay? See you later."

She waves again. "Okay, baby. You get back home before dark."

I nod and keep walking. Farther down the street, four-hundred-year-old Ms. Gibson screams at me from her rocker. Sometimes her words are slurred, so I have to listen very closely.

"Good mo'nin', Xavier. How'd you do in school?"

She can't see, either. Ms. Gibson always gets me and my brother confused. And we just had this school conversation yesterday *and* the day before. Her memory's bad, but her hearing is worse.

I scream back to her. "Made the honor roll again. And I'm Lamar."

"Oh that's won-ner-ful, just won-ner-ful! Your momma woulda been so happy. Are you eating enough fiber? You walk like you're constipated. I've got something special in the house for that if you need some assistance. Want me to go get it, Xavier?"

Two guys I go to school with pass me and chuckle. I give up just so I can leave.

"No, ma'am. I'm good. But thanks anyway. I'll

see you later, Ms. Gibson."

She didn't hear me. I can't walk fast enough. If there was another route to Striker's, I'd be all over it. I bet X doesn't get the third degree from Mrs. Ledbetter or Ms. Gibson. No way. He probably gets homemade pies brought to him with a fork and a cold glass of milk. But me, I get questions about haircuts from blind barbers and old remedies for clogged shooters. Geez. I need to bowl.

Striker's is up ahead, and I can't wait to get inside. As I cross the parking lot, I see a flyer taped to the door. *Hmm.* That wasn't there yesterday. Maybe it's about a new summer league.

I step up to the glass door and cup my hands to the sides of my face to block the sun's glare. As I lean in and read, my forehead wrinkles. My eyebrows almost touch.

What? Is this some kind of joke?

I back away and look for a prankster waiting to yell "Boo-ya!" or "Gotcha!" but it doesn't happen. I'm alone. So I step up to the glass one more time, cup my hands, and eyeball every word.

Goose bumps ripple across my skin. I begin to wheeze. Without taking my eyes off the flyer, I find my inhaler in my pocket, wrap my lips around the mouthpiece, and squish a mist down my throat. It can't be a joke! Holy guacamole!

# MEET PRO BOWLER
# BUBBA SANDERS!

6:00 P.M., JULY 4th

AT STRIKER'S BOWLING PARADISE

FUN! FIREWORKS! FREE STUFF!

YOU COULD WIN
PRO THUNDER BOWLING GEAR!

HERE'S HOW:

Write an essay of 500 words
or less on why you should win.

Send your essay to Bubba Sanders,
P.O. Box 12912, Indianapolis, IN 46228

All entries must be postmarked
by midnight, June 30th.

Four winners will be
announced at Striker's,
by Bubba Sanders, on July 4th.

I yank the front door open and step inside. Striker's is packed. Every lane is occupied. Hip-hop music blares from the speakers and rumbles through me. The hypnotic smells of hot buttered popcorn, pepperoni pizza, and burgers own the air. A bowler on lane fifteen lets go of a tight, silent spinner. His body curves as his ball turns toward the headpin.

*POW!*

Bowlers on the left and right give him props. He pumps his fist and celebrates. The music, the smells, the bowling—they're calling me because every day is party day at Striker's. I'm ready to join the fun, but first I've got to find Sergio.

"Lamar!"

I whip around. Sergio is sitting in the snack bar area with Tasha. He points toward the door. "I know you saw the flyer!"

I rush and greet him with a double fist bump. I even nod at his stuck-up girlfriend, who never speaks to me. Just to make her mad, I pull up a seat and squeeze it in between them.

"Yo, Sergio, this is crazy! I can't believe Bubba's coming to Coffin. I've got a ton of things to ask him. Do you think he'll talk to me? I've got to meet him, Sergio. You know he's my number one."

Bubba should be every bowler's number one, because he is the biggest, baddest bowler on the planet. *Bowler's Magazine* said he's the youngest dude on the Professional Bowlers Association tour to earn a million bucks. When he's rolling and ESPN covers the tournament, I'm superglued to the television. Other professional bowlers never talk trash about beating him. That's because Bubba is shut-yo'-mouth-and-sit-down good.

After he punks his competitors, kids swarm him because he hands out strawberry-flavored Bubba Gumballs to celebrate his victories. He signs autographs, shakes hands, and then, before he leaves, crosses his arms.

"What's Bubba's rule?"

"Stay in school!" they yell.

He flashes a peace sign. "Ya'll be cool."

Bubba is 6'4", with the fattest afro I've ever seen. His fro *and* his bowling ball are round mounds of perfection. I'm trying to grow a Bubba-sized fro. Mine's not a tower of power yet, and nobody else at school is sporting one, but I don't care.

Sergio raises a brow. "You're going to enter the contest, aren't you?"

I deadeye him. "Is water wet? Heck, yeah! But what's up with this essay thing? Doesn't Bubba know school's out? And June thirtieth isn't that far away."

Sergio pats me on the back. "I'm starting my essay tonight. You need to get started. You're turtle slow at writing essays. It takes you a whole year to write one sentence."

Tasha giggles. "Dang, Lamar."

I cut my eyes toward her. This conversation is between me and Sergio. She's all in my Kool-Aid and doesn't know the flavor. I'm about to say something to her when she rolls her eyes and turns her head toward the snack bar. I think, I've just found my sucker.

With tight lips and squinting eyes, I lift the black spider from my pocket and place it on the table in front of her. Sergio chuckles, and that makes her turn back to us. Her eyes hit high beam before she releases a table-shaking scream.

*"Aaaaaaaargh!"*

After she burns off toward a group of girls, I put my prize spider back in my pocket, work my eyeballs back to my boy, and drag out my words.

"An-y-way, Bubba should have given us a choice, maybe write an essay or—oh, I know—answer Bubba trivia questions to see who knows the most about him."

Sergio's still chuckling. "Tasha's going to be hot about that spider thing, Lamar."

"She needs to get in line with everybody else who's been spider-ized by the L-Train. And I'm just trying to keep up with *you*. Your fake tarantula is off the chain."

A disc-sized beeper flashes red and vibrates on the table. Sergio picks it up and grins.

"Our lane is ready. That's what's up."

I push back and stand. "No, my bowling average against yours, *that's* what's *up*."

Sergio gets in my face. "After I win, we can have a moment of silence in memory of your streak. I feel a Sergio Reyes upset in the making."

I rub my belly. "The only thing that's going to be upset is your stomach. I'll get my stuff. While you're up, loan me a couple bucks for snacks after we roll. I'll pay you back."

Sergio opens his wallet and hands me a five. "Dude, you need a job. And I know I'm never going to see this again."

I take the five. "Thanks, but you're wrong, bro. One day I'm gonna pay you back."

I pocket the money and stroll to the ball racks. Rolling with a house ball and rental shoes is "ghetto rolling" for serious bowlers. I *hate* bowling with house gear. Bubba would never roll with it. But I don't have a choice. Dad won't fork out the funds. "Things are tight right now, Lamar," he always says.

I find a ball and place it on the ball return on lane eleven. Sergio types our names into the automatic scorekeeper, then tries to rattle me.

"Check it out. This is our eleventh game, on

lane eleven, and eleven is my lucky number. Co-incidence? I think not."

I lace up my ugly brown bowling shoes and ignore him. It's time to mentally prepare for my game. That's what Bubba says in his *Bowling with Bubba* book. If it's not in his book, it's a jacked-up lie. Sergio nudges my shoulder.

"Five more days until my birthday. I can't wait."

I break my concentration and grin. "Have your parents dropped any hints?"

"Nope, but I did. I asked for a motorcycle. Probably won't get it."

I tilt my head. "Didn't you fall off your BMX last week? Training wheels is what you should have asked for. You're going to be fourteen, Sergio. Don't waste a wish on something you know you're not going to get."

He shrugs. "I just want something awesome."

I cross my arms. "Last year you got that Trickster BMX. The year before that, you got a five-hundred-dollar shopping spree at All Toys for Boys. Your parents are bankin' and you *know* they're going to get you something awesome. Let's just bowl."

Tasha rejoins us, clapping for Sergio like a battery-operated seal. I clap too, and make seal noises. *"Arr, arr, arr!"*

She stops. Sergio frowns at me.

"Cut it out, Lamar. Let's roll. I haven't got all day."

"Dang, don't get mad. I was just having some fun."

I step on the lane and lift my ball from the ball return. My middle and fourth fingers and my thumb slide into the holes and hold on. I lean forward and momentum takes over as my arm swings back and I power it forward, releasing the ball at the perfect angle. No question about it.

*POW!*

The score screen lights up. The word *STRIKE* flashes in glittery letters.

I cross my arms to form an X. "All day, baby, all day."

Sergio takes his steps and rolls a straight ball toward the center pin. I turn to Tasha.

"Did you bring bananas and ice cream? Your boy just rolled a split."

The two farthest corner pins at the back of the triangular setup are left standing. Sergio grins and shrugs. I do the same, because we both know he can't make that spare. By the tenth frame, Sergio has no possible way of catching up. So I do what Bubba would do. I shut him up and sit him down with a spare and a strike.

He grins at me. "You're really not that good, Lamar. You're just lucky."

I take the comb from my back pocket, groom my fro, and announce the score. "One-ninety-four to one-forty-two. You call it luck. I call it eleven in a row, baby, and I am still the King of Striker's."

Sergio bumps fists with me. "How do you enter the zone like that? I mean, dude, you don't even hear me when I'm talking to you. You transform into some kind of bowling zombie."

I put my comb away. "It's all in Bubba's book."

Sergio dismisses that. "I read Bubba's book twice. It's got to be something else."

"I've got one focus." I point at Tasha. "You've got one distraction."

Tasha rolls her neck from side to side and snaps her fingers. "You *wish* you had a distraction."

Sergio gives Tasha a five-dollar bill and whispers to her. She storms off toward the snack bar, but not before rolling her neck at me once more. Sergio jabs me on the shoulder.

"Lamar, you need to freeze all that hate you keep throwing at my girl." I'm speechless. As I rub my shoulder, he keeps laying it on. "That's why you'll always be a table for one. You don't know how to talk to women."

"Yes I do. Of course I do. I talk to girls all the time." I puff out my chest, but Sergio calls my bluff.

"I bet you've never held a girl's hand."

I come back hard and strong. "I'm not a

hand-holder. I'm a lip-locker. But you wouldn't know anything about lockin' lips, would you?"

Sergio leans back and grins, because he knows I busted him. "I'm working on it."

We laugh, but then my boy gets serious.

"Listen up, Lamar. Girls want superstars, smooth dudes, or bad boys. Pick one and be one. I chose smooth and look what it got me."

I push him on the shoulder. "You're not smooth."

Sergio winks. "I'm smoother than a baby's butt with lotion on it. You know it's true."

According to the hot/not polls at school, Sergio's hotter than Atomic Fireballs. No doubt about his girl mojo. Honeys call him the Spanish fly guy. I call him the luckiest dude in Coffin.

Dark hair, tan skin, cool walk, rich parents. My boy's got it going on. He drowns his curls in mousse to make them lie flat and shine. But around two o'clock those curls droop and dangle as if Sergio's growing black noodles on his forehead. It's a whole new afternoon look, and girls love that, too.

Once, I tried some of that mousse stuff in my afro. I squirted a pile of that extrahold foam in my hand and rubbed it through my hair. For ten minutes, I waited for black noodles to dangle on my forehead. Instead, my fro held an old-school slant as if me and Frederick Douglass had the same barber.

I need to flip the switch, do something to catch a girl's eye. I'm tired of being the third wheel with Sergio and Tasha. I hate sitting with them at the movies or tagging along at the mall.

If Sergio can have a fine girl, I can, too. I'll do anything to get a honey. If girls want superstars, smoothies, or bad boys, I'll be the most athletic, smoothest, baddest dude in Coffin.

## Chapter Three

We're about to start our second game when Sergio clears the score and rubs his head.

"I'm getting a headache."

I give him my most serious face. "Do you have a penny?"

He reaches in his pocket and pulls one out. "Why?"

"I hear there's something in copper that heals head pain. But the copper has to be, uh . . . warm. Give me that penny. I'll warm it and bring it back."

Sergio hands me his coin and I detour to the front desk. I ask for a pencil. After looking over my shoulder to be sure Sergio's not watching, I scribble heavy pencil lead across the edge of the penny. I hurry back to Sergio and hope my face doesn't give anything away.

"Does it still hurt?"

He winces. "Yeah, a little."

"Here, this should help."

I roll the coin across his forehead, from one ear to the other, back and forth, three times, leaving lines of dark pencil marking as I roll. When I finish, Sergio's forehead resembles blank sheet music.

"Feeling better yet?"

He nods. "Yeah, I do. Wow. Copper. Who knew? Thanks, bro."

I've got a glob of laugh-out-loud hiding in my throat. "Sure. No problem."

I'm ready to whip his butt for the twelfth time in a row when Billy Jenks drops his bag in a seat on the lane to the right of us. Two teenage dudes carrying bowling bags follow him. Billy's arguing with them, and judging by the cursing and the glares, I figure someone's going to throw a punch soon. I've got ringside seats and refuse to budge. Sergio pulls up next to me and we listen to one of those chumps go off on Billy.

"I don't care about the guy who backed out, Billy. You promised us a two-on-two match. My brother won't be back to pick me up for an hour.

You need to find somebody to roll with you or I'm going to act a fool up in here."

I'm ready to watch them duke it out until three fine girls from school step into the bowlers' area to the left. I nudge my boy, and since Tasha's not here, we check out the honeys together. Sergio thinks I don't have game, but I do, and now is the perfect time to prove it. I rub my chin like I've got hair growing on it and wink at them.

"You girls going to bowl?"

Sergio chuckles and whispers, "Why else would they be wearing bowling shoes? That sure made you look stupid."

I glance at the pencil lines across his forehead. He's pimpin' a whole new level of dork and doesn't even know it. I declare myself Prince of Prank and celebrate by nodding my head to the music.

Even though I keep talking to those fine females, they don't answer me.

"If you ladies need any help, let me know."

Nothing.

How can I make them see the real Lamar? I'm not about jokes all the time. I can be serious.

Oh no.

I cut my eyes to Sergio and wonder if the honeys watched me draw lines on his forehead. They probably did. Way to act like a serious guy, Lamar.

I shuffle over to a seat in the bowlers' area and

park. I'm so invisible to girls. This may be a long, lonely summer if I don't figure out how to switch things up. I bend to retie my shoes, but Billy's angry voice startles me.

"I understand! Just give me a minute!"

I've known Billy Jenks since kindergarten. He's tall on attitude but short in stature. Billy's so low to the ground, I bet his hair and feet smell the same. I'd never seen a person with a square face until I saw his. It's all smashed in, like he got clocked with a can of Spam.

But every kid in Coffin knows Billy Jenks equals trouble. Rumors say he's a gold-card member of juvenile detention. I know he's done time in three boot camps and he's only fourteen. Other than seeing each other at Striker's or at school, we don't mix.

He glances toward the door, shakes his head, and calls off the game. One of the dudes cups his hand to his mouth and blasts, "Coffin bowlers are chumps."

It's one thing to talk about the dude who didn't show up. But this punk has just called out our whole town. I shove my hands into my pockets, step closer, and speak before I even realize I've done it.

"What's going on, Jenks?"

Billy turns, and I lock in on the iciest blue eyes

in the universe. "Hey, Washington. These guys are trying to chump Coffin bowlers. Can you believe it?"

I snatch my inhaler, shake it, and press the canister until I hear the swish. As the spray goes down my throat, I shove my inhaler back into my pocket like it's a high-powered weapon. "You need a bowler?"

Billy's eyebrows jump. "For real? I'll pay for your game if you roll with me."

I pop my knuckles. Sergio whispers in my ear.

"No. You are *not* for real. Snap out of it! It's Billy Jenks, fool!"

He's right. I fake a concerned look at my watch, and just as I fix my mouth to say "My bad, I lost track of time," a honey made of the finest brown sugar sashays by. With a gym bag on her shoulder, she wipes her face with a towel and glides into the lane on the left with those other three girls.

Her tight, ocean blue soccer shirt has me seasick. Black shorts, blue socks, and black-and-blue Nikes show me the girl's got style. She's got braids swishing on her shoulders and my neck sways with them. Only one word can describe this goddess from the island of sexy soccer.

"Dang."

I keep looking and swaying. Suddenly, she looks at me. My neck locks. Holy crackers and cream cheese! I'm stuck in stupid. Jenks snaps his fingers and I flinch.

"What's the verdict, Washington? Are you Coffin proud or what?"

As my eyes ping-pong from Jenks to the soccer princess, Sergio grabs my arm.

"Can I talk to you a minute? Alone?" he asks.

I nod. "Yeah, but it will have to wait. You've got something on your forehead, bro. You better go check it out in the men's room." I turn to Billy. "Let's roll."

While Billy pays for my game, another quick glance confirms that the soccer princess is watching. I pimp my walk just to prove confidence is not an issue with me. Near the ball return, a sparkle makes me look. I'm mesmerized by the shiniest green Bubba Sanders Pro Thunder I've ever seen.

"Who's rolling with that?"

Billy steps back into the bowler's area. "I am."

I get close and see BILLY J. engraved above the finger holes. I sure hope he doesn't disgrace Bubba and roll gutter balls.

I sneak another peek at the soccer princess. She looks my way. I nod at her. She doesn't nod back. I lift my hand to wave, but Billy stands in front of me and short-circuits my love connection.

"Lamar, this is Jesse Ray and Robert Earl from Scottsburg."

I've seen these guys at the mall. Jesse's got a Peyton Manning jersey on. He blows a monster bubble, and I want to pop it all over his face.

Robert Earl has braces, a mop of red hair, and a face full of freckles. He's sporting green high-cut girly shorts with green Converse Chuck Taylors and a green-and-white shirt. All that red and green reminds me of a big bag of holiday M&Ms.

I turn to Billy. "Let's rock and bowl."

Billy rolls first. I watch his form. He obviously hasn't read Bubba's book. He gets six pins on the first ball, two on the second. Jesse Ray's next.

Jesse takes his time, pulls his weapon from the ball return, and faces the pins. Still and patient as a king cobra, he waits. The bowlers' area is quiet. I'm nervous. This guy has skills.

He takes a step, then another. His ball swings behind him, high in the air, and shifts forward as he releases it before the foul line. It rolls close to the edge of the gutter and I'm ready to laugh until it takes a wicked cut to the left. It's the nastiest curve I've seen in a long time.

*POW!*

He turns, pops another big bubble, and stares at me with a half grin. I've got something for you, bubblehead boy. I snatch my house ball and ease up to the approach line.

I won't even look at the pins. It's not time. My

shoes touch as I position myself to roll something filthy. My fingers grip inside the holes and I lift the ball to my side. I close my eyes and enter the zone. *Now* it's time.

My eyelids lift slowly and zero in on my real opponent. Sixty feet away ten pin-shaped soldiers double dare me to take them down. They stand at attention in a tight triangle, but I'm not intimidated. My right foot leads the charge.

As my left foot follows, both hands push the ball away. My left hand lets go, leaving two fingers and a thumb on my right hand to take care of business. I find my rhythm, swing that ball back, then throw a Coffin-sized stink bomb down the lane.

I turn around and strut back to my seat before my ball reaches the pins.

*BLAM!*

Billy makes an X with his arms. I make an X, too, then turn to Jesse.

"This Coffin bowling chump is going to whip your bubble-blowing rump."

I take a seat and steal another look at my goddess of soccer. She's laughing and bowling. Our eyes meet. I get bold and smile. She doesn't smile back. But at least she sees me.

Billy cleans the left gutter on his next turn. I'm ready to call the bowling police. It should be against the law what he's doing to his Bubba's Pro

Thunder. Robert Earl gets five pins on both rolls. He bowls more like the green M&M than the red one. Jesse tries to keep up with me, but I'm rolling with a bigger purpose. This is my house, my bowling alley, and I want that message on the scorer's sheet.

By the seventh frame, I take on Jesse Ray as if Bubba had invaded my body. I shut that fool up and sit him down with a score of 186 to his 159. Billy scores a 147 to Robert Earl's 112.

I lift my hands in the air and put their butts on blast.

"From Coffin to grave, baby, from Coffin to grave!"

They don't appreciate my humor, and Jesse lets me know it.

"You need to shut up, Washington. Or we can take this outside," he says.

Doesn't he know I've got a girl watching me? So I push him. I'm about to break my fist off in his eye when Jenks steps between us.

"You got a problem, Jesse?"

Jesse backs away. "No, Billy. I'm just ready to get out of here."

"Fine. Be gone." Billy turns to me. "I'll be back. Don't leave."

They shuffle through the exit doors. Jesse gives me one more look. I nod at him, hit my chest twice with my fist, and shoot him a peace sign.

"Don't let the doorknob hit you where my house ball bit you!"

The soccer goddess moves to a table behind us to remove her bowling shoes. Her friends leave but promise to call her later. She looks my way again, and I'm about to wink at her when I see Sergio walking my way. He plops down beside me. His face smells like soap.

"I can't believe I fell for that. My forehead looked like school paper. But I have to admit it was funny."

I burst into laughter, but Sergio calms me down with a hand on my shoulder.

"That girl's checking you out. It's time to make a move."

I push his hand away. "What are you? Crazy?"

He puts his hand back on my shoulder. "I double dare you with cheese to talk to her."

Sergio backs me into a corner with the double dare. After beating Jesse Ray and Robert Earl, instead of feeling invisible, I feel invincible. So I take the challenge.

"She's mine. Stand back and watch the master at work."

# Chapter Four

My feet switch to autowalk. I'm halfway there when I realize Mom never got a chance to talk to me about girls before she died. Dad has never showed me how to bust a move. X tells me I'll never get a girl because I'm swamp scum. I'm probably about to get my face slappa-lappa-jacked by the finest honey I've ever seen, and it's all Sergio's fault for daring me.

I slow my pace and look over my shoulder. Sergio's still watching. I can't detour to the men's room. I shouldn't have taken that dare. She won't talk to me. This girl is grade-A, high-quality fine, like queens and supermodels. I'm inching toward her. She's watching me. Dang.

I've made my way to her table. She looks scared. I grab the top of the empty chair.

"Uh, hi. Is this seat taken? I mean . . . can I sit here?"

She looks at all the empty tables and chairs in the snack bar, then back at me. I feel a neck roll coming, followed by two finger snaps and a verbal beat-down. Please don't crack my face in front of Sergio.

But she shrugs. "It's a free country."

I slide the chair back and sit but don't scoot in, just in case I need to dash. Okay, round one is in the books. The score is Lamar—one; superfine girl—zero.

Round two is my specialty. It's time to give her a glimpse of the L-Train.

"Uh, wow, your braids are bangin'. I've never seen them that thin before. They look like . . . uh . . . like a thousand baby snakes."

She scoots her chair back. Oh no! She's going to bounce! I scramble for a correction.

"Not poisonous ones! Snakes rock! Hey, don't leave. Okay, I take it back."

That was a bad round. I'm going to give her a point for staying. Now for the final round. Come on, Lamar, you can do it. Stop all of this jabbing and go for the knockout.

I lean back in my chair. "So, do you love bowling?"

She leans forward. "Why are you talking to me, Lamar?"

Holy guacamole, she sucker punched me! How'd she know my name? I've never even seen her before. No way I would have forgotten those gorgeous light brown eyes.

I Google my memory, but it returns the message *Your search did not match any documents.* Great. I'm clueless. It must show in my face, because she gives me a tiny hint.

"We've gone to the same schools since day care," she says.

I send that piece of info to my memory and try again. It Scrabbles up, down, and across, but it won't spell out her name. And how am I supposed to remember who I went to day care with?

She crosses her arms. "Makeda? Makeda Phillips? Dang, Lamar."

I lean forward for a closer look and freak. "Fivehead Makeda?"

Everybody knows Makeda Phillips has the tallest forehead in the galaxy. There must be a full five inches of naked skin from her eyebrows to her hairline. She definitely has a fivehead, not a forehead like the rest of us.

I've never noticed anything but her temple of

dome in the past. But her bangs hide that fivehead pretty good. I enjoy the view until it dawns on me she's still not smiling.

"I didn't mean to call you, well, you know. You look so . . ."

Her eyebrows rise and disappear under her bangs. "Different?"

I smile. "Exactly. In a really good way."

"Thank you, but you still haven't answered my question. Why are you talking to me?"

Why do girls ask hard questions? I'm struggling to answer when she shocks me.

"I know you've got some prank in the making. You and Sergio always do." She starts to get up. "But I'm not falling for them anymore. See you later."

I show her my hands. "No pranks, I swear. I just want to talk to you. Please don't leave. Hey, isn't Makeda the name of a famous queen?"

A slight half grin forms as she sits back down. "Yeah. My parents named me after the queen of Sheba. I didn't think anybody knew her real name was Makeda."

I exhale. Whoa. That was close. What a save! I put one hand in my pocket and strike a pose.

"You look a whole lot better than the queen of Sheba. She's all ashes to ashes, dust to dust. Deader than disco, know what I mean?"

Judging by the look on Makeda's face, I've just slid from Mac Daddy to Whack Dudley. If I could get my foot up high enough, I'd kick my own butt. I pull my hand out of my pocket, and the five dollars Sergio gave me falls to the carpet. I glance back at her.

"Let me buy you a Coke or something from the snack bar, as an apology. I was stupid. Come on. You gotta give me a second chance."

She tilts her head. "Is this apology for putting a tack in my chair in science lab, for high-fiving my forehead in the cafeteria, or for all the rude things you've ever said to me?"

Wow. Better make that a large Coke. I bite my lip, scrunch my eyebrows, and rub my face searching for a really good answer. When I glance across the table, she's grinning.

"I guess I'm a little thirsty. I'll wait for a few minutes, but I'm not going to let you pull that old 'waiting forever' prank on me again."

Holy crackers and cream cheese, that was a classic! My teeth clamp to stop the big glob of laugh-out-loud creeping up my throat. It happened back at the beginning of seventh grade. Sergio told Makeda I had a crush on her and wanted to hook up after school. When the bell rang, me and Sergio rushed outside, hid behind some bushes, and timed her. She waited thirty whole minutes. I laughed for days.

I mentally check back in and glance at Makeda across the table. She's blinking and thinking, staring at her fingers with a sad, sad face. *Hmm.* Didn't she think it was funny? I never thought about how she felt about that prank. Now it's not so funny.

I get up and cross my heart with my pointer. "I swear. No more pranks. Just don't leave."

She checks her watch. "Then you better hurry."

I rush to the snack bar and order two Cokes plus a bag of popcorn. Sergio pulls up.

"Way to go, Romeo. What's her name? She's new, isn't she?"

I break the news. "Dude, it's Makeda Phillips."

Sergio's eyes widen. "Fivehead? Quit playing."

We both take a slow look over our shoulders before turning back around.

"Dang, Lamar, she sure disguised herself with that new hairstyle. That's kind of scary. Good thing you didn't promise her anything."

I look at Sergio again. He rolls his eyes.

"What did you promise her?"

I shrug. "Just a Coke."

The snack bar guy rings me up. "Six dollars."

I turn to Sergio. "I'm a buck short. Can I borrow one more from you?"

He frowns. "Dude, step away from the snack

bar. It's Fivehead. Hey, I've got an idea. Leave her sitting there. That'll be hilarious."

"I promised her, no more pranks. And I can't just dump her."

Sergio gives the snack bar guy another buck, then turns to me.

"I didn't know you were *that* desperate. I'm taking Tasha to the movies. I'll call you tonight, and hopefully you'll tell me she's history."

I grab the Cokes and popcorn. "Later, bro. Thanks for the cash."

Sergio's words sting. I'm not desperate. I'm handling my business. Bump him. A superfine girl is talking to me, and I don't care what she *used* to look like.

I strut back to the table and she's still there.

"Here's your Coke. I got popcorn, too."

"Thanks."

I hold up my drink. "Let's toast to a new start, okay?"

Our cups touch, but her expression worries me. I don't think she buys this whole "no more pranks" thing.

Makeda takes a sip of her Coke and I chuck a few pieces of popcorn in my mouth. What can I ask her? What can I tell her? Man, this conversation thing is tough, so I say the first thing that comes to my mind.

"Do you just bowl to hang out with your friends?"

She takes a sip of her drink. "No. I love bowling. I'm here almost every day. "

I almost choke on my popcorn. "No way! I bowl every day, too. Why haven't I seen you?"

I know the answer and wish I hadn't asked her to remind me how much of a jerk I've been. Lucky for me, she stays quiet, so I change the subject.

"Did you get a bowling pass?"

I offer her popcorn. She takes some and admits, "Yeah, I got one."

"You got your pass with you right now?"

She stops chewing and stands. I rewind what I just asked, searching for clues of stupidity. She blinks hard at me. With both hands on her hips, she rolls her neck from side to side and I wonder if she has any bones in that thing.

"Oh, I get it. You want my free games, right? I should have seen that coming. Use up Makeda's free games and then laugh at her."

I spill popcorn all over the table as I hold both hands toward her. "No, that's not what I meant. I just thought we could bowl a game together or something, because I've got my pass, too. See? I've still got one game left. Honest."

She checks out my pass and shakes her head. "I have to go."

I stand, too. "Will you be here tomorrow?"

She lifts her soccer bag. "I don't know, maybe. Bye, Lamar. Thanks for the Coke."

I watch her leave. Dang it! I didn't get her phone number. It's not too late. I take a step from the table and bump into Billy Jenks.

"Washington, can I talk to you a minute?"

I shake him off. "Not now, Billy."

Two crisp twenties brush across my wrist and land on the table. My eyes bulge, and I turn back to him. He crosses his arms.

"They're yours. You want 'em or what?"

I hesitate to touch the money. "What's the catch?"

"There's no catch in my game, Washington. Forty bucks is chump change to me. It should be to you, too. If you're interested in making some serious cash, grab a seat."

I look toward the door. She's gone. I glance at the twenties and then at Billy. He plops into the chair Makeda has just emptied.

"Let's talk business, Washington."

I ease back down and keep my eyes on Billy. He's grinning at me.

"Wow, talk about impressive. You really *are* the King of Striker's."

"Thanks."

"I'm serious. I mean, at school you're geek of

the week or something, no offense. But here, I don't know, you're awesome."

"Yeah, well, I gotta bounce."

I get up and Billy rubs his hands together.

"I just ordered a pepperoni pizza for us. You down? It's just my way of saying thanks. You saved my butt today."

I quick sit. Striker's pizza is off the chain.

"Yeah, I guess I can stay a minute."

He taps on the table. "And by the way, your brother is an awesome basketball player."

I shrug. "He's a'ight."

Billy chuckles. "Are you kidding me? He's an all-star. I bet he gets a scholarship."

I look around Striker's. "Can we talk about something else?"

He leans back in his chair and stares at me. "Sure. No problem. I wish I could talk about *my* brother's basketball skills, but he stinks. And Dad thinks he's the next Larry Bird."

I bring my focus back to Billy. He shrugs and keeps talking.

"Yeah, Dad's all into Scooter's basketball career, so I've got my own thing going on. When I need new gear, I go buy it myself. Has your dad ever bought you bowling gear?"

My eyes lower. "No."

"Hey, have you ever noticed how our dads sit

together at the basketball games? Seems like they've got a lot in common. What do you think?"

I don't answer. Where's that pizza? I glance over my shoulder and see a round flat pan coming our way. Once it's on the table, Billy and I dig in. I've got a mouth full of pizza when he starts talking crazy.

"I saw you checking out my Pro Thunder. Sweet, isn't it? Want one?"

I nod toward the posters. "Bubba's giving four of 'em away. One has my name on it, hands down, no questions asked. I'm his number one and my essay will be off the chain."

Billy grabs another slice. "You need to man up, Washington. How many essays do you think Bubba's going to get?"

"I don't know, maybe a few hundred."

"At least. So think about it. The odds are against you. Do the math."

I cross my arms. "I don't see anything wrong with writing an essay, Billy."

"You know, Washington, with your bowling skills, you should have butt-kickin' bowling gear and a fat roll of cash in your wallet. I'm not nearly as good as you are and I keep a stash."

I shake my head. "I don't bowl for money."

"Oh, I forgot. You're counting on an essay

miracle. If you ever want better odds, holler at me. I could use you on my team. How does fifty bucks a game sound to you?"

My eyes bulge again as my jaws stop chewing. "You mean real cash?"

He opens his wallet to show a layer of green. "Does this look like Monopoly money?"

I raise one eyebrow. "How'd you get that?"

He snaps his wallet closed and stuffs it in his back pocket. "I work the lanes. There's always somebody ready to bet on a game."

I choose my words carefully. "No offense, Billy, but you're not that good."

He chuckles. "I sandbagged. Jesse Ray and Robert Earl—they didn't need to see my best stuff. When you rolled that first strike, I decided to roll gutter balls. The next time we bowl against them, they'll look for you and I'll roll fire. You gotta know how to play the game."

I lean back. "Don't you ever play for fun? I mean, you know, for free?"

He looks right at me. "I don't do anything for free. I'm a businessman, Washington. Don't ever forget that. Everything I do is about banking. That's why you got paid. I had money on that game, and you came through for me."

Both of my eyebrows rise. "There's something

illegal about this, isn't there?"

Jenks chuckles. "Of course not. I'm legit. Check it out."

He pulls out a business card and chucks it across the table to me. I pick it up and freak.

---

BILLY M. JENK$

812-555-9090

*Money is my middle name*

---

"Dang, Billy, you've got business cards? Is 'Money' really your middle name?"

"No, it's Michael, but the card bangs, doesn't it?"

"Yeah."

I open my hand and stare at the twenties. I can't remember when I've ever held this much money and it didn't belong to my doctor or the grocery store. Billy keeps talking.

"I bet every essay Bubba reads has 'Bubba, I'm your number-one fan' in the opening line. Come on, Washington, think about it. Most of these bowlers never cared about or even heard of Bubba until his picture and 'free gear' appeared on that flyer. Pro bowlers don't get props like basketball and football stars. Be honest. Had you heard a lot of people talking about Bubba? I mean before the flyer went up?"

"No."

Billy leans in. "Heck no. They're all posers, using him just to get something free. If you write an essay, he'll think you're just the same as them. You want to impress Bubba? Own a Pro Thunder before he gets here. Bubba's a businessman, too. He'll respect you because you're not looking for a freebie. Understand?"

I try to defend myself. "But I'm pretty good at writing. . . ."

"Writing essays is for chumps. A real man drops cash on the counter for what he wants. My way to a Pro Thunder is guaranteed."

I try to sort things out. My internal stink sensor is going berserk, but he's right. I don't want Bubba thinking I'm looking for a handout. I'm deep in thought when Billy pushes back his chair and wipes his mouth with his sleeve.

"Time's up. You blew a prime opportunity, Washington. Good luck with the essay."

I tighten my grip on the money. "Wait! Okay, I'm listening—what do I have to do?"

He scoots back to the table and puts his wallet

away. "It's easy. Do what you did today. We win, you make fifty bucks. We lose, it costs you nothing. I'll cover our losses. We'll be partners."

I rub the top of my head. "I'm feeling weird about this."

"That weird feeling is having cash in your pocket to buy a Pro Thunder or take a girl to the movies when she wants to go. I saw you rapping to Makeda Phillips. She's hot. How are you going to pay for movies, concerts, and stuff like that?"

A cell phone rings and Billy takes it from his shirt pocket. He checks the caller ID.

"I've got to take this call. My number is on the card. If you want in, you better hurry before I find someone else. I'm not leaving this offer on the table forever. Later, Washington."

I wait for him to leave before letting out the glob of excitement stuck in my throat.

It's time to celebrate! I've still got one game left on my bowling pass, and I'm ready to use it. Holy guacamole, luck doubled up on me today! Money *and* a possible honey!

Sergio's never going to believe this!

# Chapter Five

It's five thirty when I finish rolling my last game and head to the house. I've got pep in my step, but I slow down to wave at Mrs. Ledbetter as she sweeps her driveway.

"On my way home, Mrs. Ledbetter."

"You're a good boy, Lamar. See you tomorrow."

Ms. Gibson's head is bowed. She snores so hard that her chair rocks every time she inhales. I keep walking and don't disturb her. A few minutes later, I'm taking our porch steps two at a time.

When I open the front door, my nose flares as smothered-pork-chops vapors drift into my nose and welcome me home. I'm heading straight for the table when Dad comes from the kitchen. He's not smiling.

"Go wash up for dinner."

"Yes, sir. Smells good, Dad."

Seems like the three of us get to the dinner table and slide into our chairs at the same time. Dad prays and right after that, we get busy. The only sound is clean pork chop bones falling to our plates. Dad's very quiet, and I keep my eye on him. I'm ready for my third chop when X tells Dad I did a bum job cleaning the bathroom.

If I could fling a bone across the table and dot Xavier's eye, I would. Instead, I let it slip that Xavier sneaks girls into the house when Dad goes to work. I get a nasty look from my brother. He gets one back.

Dad's fork slams to his plate. X and I jump.

"I can't deal with this right now, boys. I've got much bigger problems to handle."

Xavier speaks for both of us. "What's wrong, Dad? Tell us. Maybe we can help."

He looks at the family portrait on the wall. "They cut my hours today. Things are going to get even tighter than they are. I need you boys to hang tough, keep costs low by turning off lights, maybe eating a little less. Just for a while."

"Sure, Dad," I say.

Xavier tries to lighten the mood. "I thought it

was something horrible! Don't worry, Dad. We'll be all right. Let me tell you about this new play we learned for the game."

While X gets Dad involved in a basketball conversation, I put my third pork chop back on the serving tray. I'm suddenly full and wondering how I can help.

Maybe it wasn't a coincidence that Billy offered me a job. I could roll with him, get my new gear, and even help Dad out. That's it!

My thoughts switch again, but this time to station MKDA. It's ugly-duckling crazy how Fivehead has morphed into a hottie. I push away from the table to go think about her some more in my room when Dad looks my way. I know what that means. Here comes my two-minute drill.

"Did you take your meds?"

"Yes, sir."

"When's your next doctor's appointment?"

"I haven't made an appointment yet."

"Sergio okay?"

"Yes, sir."

"How'd you bowl today?"

"Good."

That's it. We're done. The phone rings and I race to get it. I know it's Sergio. He calls every night at this same time. I take the phone to my room and start talking.

"Dude, you're not going to believe what happened to me today."

Sergio whispers, "Wait, *you're* never going to believe what I heard my parents talking about a few minutes ago."

I close my door. "Does it have anything to do with your birthday?"

"It has everything to do with it. They're making plans to drop me off at Holiday World. And get this—they're not staying. They're gonna let me take a friend and spend the whole day!"

I flop on the bed. "No way! I know you're going to take me, aren't you?"

"Of course! Remember the last time we went? Holiday World has the nastiest wooden roller coaster on the planet, but you couldn't ride it because you were wheezing."

I sit up. "This time, I'll take extra medicine. And I'll eat two hot dogs with mustard, catsup, and relish before I get on it. And I won't puke. Can you top that?"

"I'll eat that and chug a chocolate milk shake. I can't wait."

I begin to pace. "Me neither. It's going to be awesome."

"So what did you want to tell me?"

"Check this out, Sergio. After you left with

Tasha, Billy Jenks dropped forty bucks on the table. I got paid for bowling with him against those chumps from Scottsburg."

"You bowled for money?"

"Yeah, and I didn't even know it."

There's a weird silence in our connection. "Yo, Sergio, are you still there?"

"Yeah, I'm here. Aren't you a little worried Billy's going to want something else from you? I can't believe he paid you and that's it."

"Don't worry. I had a long conversation with him."

Sergio lets out a huge sigh. "If you say so. Have you started your essay?"

Here we go. This is it. I close my eyes, scratch the top of my fro, and break the news.

"I'm not writing one. I've found another way to get a Pro Thunder."

"How? Is your dad buying you one?"

I think about Dad's bad luck and know I'm making the right choice.

"Billy made me his partner. I'm going to roll with him this summer. I'm talking crazy mad cash, Sergio. Told you I'd pay you back. I've got it right now."

There's more silence than an unplugged telephone. Then Sergio comes down hard.

"I don't want *that* money! I can't believe this! What's wrong with you?"

"Nothing, except I'm tired of begging for money. You should be happy for me."

"I would be happy if you had a *real* job."

"It *is* a real job! And while I'm telling you stuff, I didn't give Makeda the boot."

Now the silence gets ugly. I hear hard air pushing out of Sergio's nose before he unloads again.

"You're not thinking, bro. Billy's been in and out of juvie since he was born. Fivehead is the easiest joke in school. Your reputation is heading downhill instead of up. Is that what you want?"

I fire back. "Billy's never done anything to me. And her name is Makeda."

"This is the worst news ever! I've got a bad feeling. You better watch yourself. Don't ever say I didn't warn you."

"Whatever, Sergio. There's not going to be any drama. I'll talk to you later."

"Yeah, whatever, Lamar."

I slam the phone down. My left eye twitches. My teeth clamp. Then I remember Sergio's never worked for anything in his life. The phone rings again and this time, I pick it up and blast him.

"No need to call me back, because you're not going to change my mind."

"Is this Lamar?"

"Is this Sergio?"

"No, this is Billy. I've got us a gig tomorrow. We bowl at eleven thirty. Is that cool?"

I drop my attitude down a few notches before answering.

"Yeah, it's cool. I'll be there."

"Excellent. Later, Washington."

"Yeah, later, Billy."

I hang up, open my closet, and grab the empty shoe box that my Jordans came in. I toss the two twenties inside and place it back on the shelf. I made forty bucks in less than an hour. If I keep this up, I'll have my Pro Thunder before Sergio gets a stamp on his essay envelope. If Billy keeps lining up games, even after I get my ball, I'll have thousands of dollars left over.

I snatch my sunglasses off my desk, slide them on, and stare at myself in the mirror. I pretend my arm is around Makeda's shoulder at the mall and she's looking at jewelry.

"You want the diamond earrings in the window? Go ahead and get 'em, baby. And let's buy the electric company for my dad so he won't have to worry about that bill ever again. I can do all that and more, because I own the Bank of Lamar."

Yeah. That's what's up.

## Chapter Six

$\mathcal{F}$riday morning the garbage truck roars down the street. I grab the trash and open the door. Dad shuffles by.

"Where are you going?"

"I finished my chores. I'm going to Striker's."

He yawns. "Hey, wait. I know things are a little tight, but on my next day off, let's hit the lanes, okay? You and me."

I shrug. "Sure, okay. Later, Dad."

Just as I open the door he calls to me.

"Don't forget about your brother's basket-ball game. I'm leaving at four o'clock. We can go together. You did your breathing exercises, didn't you?"

"Yes, sir. See you later."

I wish I had more time to talk with Dad, but it's already eleven twenty-five. Billy might be mad if I'm late. I drop the trash at the curb and get moving. Mrs. Ledbetter isn't outside, so that's a plus. Ms. Gibson is asleep again, so I ease on by. Five minutes later, I yank the door to Striker's and the cool breeze greets me. I'm sweaty and hope my shirt doesn't stain in the armpits. I get my rental shoes, and while I search for a ball, someone taps my shoulder. It's Billy.

"You're right on time, Washington."

He's standing next to two dudes who look familiar. Both guys have my skin color and Sergio's dark shiny hair.

Billy introduces us. "Lamar, this is Sandeep and Omar."

I nod. "Yeah, I know. You guys started school way late, didn't you?"

Both stare as Sandeep answers. "Bowling."

Billy nudges me and chuckles. "You ready?"

"I guess."

Sandeep and Omar aren't bad. I watch them practice while I prepare the way Bubba's book tells me. Billy puts our names in the computerized scorekeeper and the game begins. They both spare their first frame by knocking down a few on the first try and getting the rest on their second. When it's Billy's turn, he gets up, grabs his Pro Thunder, strolls to the lane, and throws a gutter ball. He shakes his hand as if something hurt.

"Ball slipped," he says.

I keep my eye on him. He turns my way and winks.

"Okay, hold us up, Lamar."

I turn to answer and notice Sergio and Tasha seated at a table behind lane ten, not far from Makeda.

Makeda! When did she get here? Oh, no.

I look past the bowlers' area. Sergio glances at the lane, then back at me. He says something to Tasha, and they move to a snack bar table. I know Billy's sandbagging again. Maybe Sergio knows he is, too. But that's not my fault. I never fake the funk when I bowl, and Sergio shouldn't blame me for what Billy does.

*BLAM!*

We spank Omar and Sandeep, but they take it like good sports. After we shake hands, Billy heads toward the exit with them. He turns back to me.

"Stick around and I'll have something for you in a minute."

"Okay."

I wait by the exit door for Billy but keep my eyes on Makeda. Sergio's staring a hole in my face, but I won't look his way. I feel bad enough about Billy's gutter balls.

Moments later, Billy steps inside and signals me to follow him. He pushes the door to the men's room and stops in the middle of the floor. He scans the place before taking a roll of dough from his pocket.

"Awesome again! Here's your cut: fifty bucks. You've made ninety bucks in two days for two hours of work. Now where are you going to find a job that pays that kind of money? Still want to write that essay?"

He stands there, holding the door and nodding. "I know you weren't down with my bowling today. But I knew you could carry us. Keep doing what I tell you and you won't regret it. That's a for-sure bet, Washington. Oh, I've got something for you."

He reaches in his pocket and tosses a cell phone to me.

"There's limited minutes on that phone. It's for us to communicate and that's it, okay? It's set on vibrate, so it won't ring and you won't have to explain the new phone. Partners need to stay in touch, right? You're a good partner, Washington."

I've never had a cell phone. It's silver and fits in

my palm. "Thanks."

I follow him out of the rest room and stuff the phone into my pocket. He turns left and I turn right toward Makeda's table. She's decked out in pink shorts with a pink-and-white blouse and a pink headband. I stop and smile at her.

"Hi."

She grins back. I lean against the table and get my mac on.

"Girl, you look like a big piece of Bubblicious."

Her grin fades, and so does mine when I realize she didn't take that as a compliment.

"I love gum. It's just you're all pink and . . . my bad, Makeda."

I take a seat and avoid direct eye contact with her, but she busts me anyway.

"What's Billy doing? I've seen his game. Gutters aren't a part of it. He was sandbagging, wasn't he? Are you two hustling? Don't try to play me."

I shrug. "He's trying something new. Please don't go all lecture on me, okay?"

"I wasn't. I just asked a question."

The wonderful aroma of cheese and pepperoni drifts in my nostrils. The perfect conversation changer suddenly comes to me.

"Want some pepperoni pizza? I'll buy."

Makeda grins. "That sounds good."

I get up, take a few steps, and turn back to her.

"And your outfit is fly."

She's still grinning. "Thanks."

Holy pepperoni! It's hard to strut and move through crowds, especially when you've got money and an awesome cell phone in your pocket. But I try anyway. Back up, suckers! I'm buying a girl something to eat. That's right, I said *a girl*, and she's hungry. Don't make me call somebody, because I've got a cell phone.

I get us a large pizza with extra cheese, place it on the table and take a big whiff.

"*Mmmm.* Doesn't that smell good?"

Makeda's eyes sparkle as she takes a piece. "Yes, it really does. I haven't had pizza since school let out."

I stop in midchew. "Why?"

"We don't eat pizza at our house. Mom cooks every day, and pizza never makes the menu."

I wipe my mouth with my wrist. "Well, you can have a slice of pizza every day if you want. I'll make sure of it."

I'm thinking that's a great hint of my intentions. But by the look on her face, it wasn't.

I shrug. "What? What did I say?"

"Lamar, why are you doing this? What do you want?"

"Nothing. I just . . . what do I have to do to make you believe that I'm through with pranks?"

She plays with her bangs. "I don't know. I want to believe you, but my brain reminds me I'm eating pizza with the guy who made me hate going to school."

I pick up my drink and look in it to hide my face. "I made a mistake. People can change."

When she doesn't answer, I raise my eyes to meet hers. We hold that gaze and I don't look away. I want her to see it in my eyes, hear it in my voice, and know I mean it. Finally, she breaks our silence.

"The pizza's good. Thanks."

I smile back. "What are your plans for the summer?"

"MVP camp."

I should've asked something else. This girl's way out of my league. She's probably got fifteen MVP trophies with little golden ladies posing on her fireplace mantel. When she finds out my hardware count is zilch, she'll kick me to the curb. So I might as well act like it's no big deal.

"What did you get your MVP trophy for? Soccer?"

She giggles. "Oh no. MVP stands for 'morals, values, and principles.' It's a camp right outside of Evansville. This is my third summer attending, and I'm being considered for a position as assistant counselor. I'm pumped about it."

"Is it for guys and girls?"

"Just girls. But it's the best four days of my summer. There are lots of girls from all over Indiana. It's the one place where I can be myself."

"What do you mean?"

She shakes her head. "You'll laugh."

"No I won't."

Makeda puts those big brown eyes on me. I give her my full attention.

"My grandmother was a missionary. She devoted her life to helping people. Mom and I traveled with her once to a very poor area in Mexico. I'll never forget the friends I made and how many times the people thanked us for coming. I can't imagine doing anything else."

I nod. "That sounds tight."

"It was. The girls around here . . . I mean, they're my friends and everything, but I can't share my dream with them. They'll think I'm weird."

I shrug. "So MVP camp teaches you how to be a missionary?"

She shrugs. "Yeah, that's probably a good way to put it. We learn how to care about ourselves and how to care for others."

I lift my drink toward my mouth and try to find the straw with my lips and accidentally stick it up my nose, which tickles and makes me sneeze all over the pizza.

"*Eew*—Lamar!"

I wipe my hand across the remaining pieces. "My bad. I'll order us another one."

"No, two pieces was plenty."

I set the pizza on the table next to us. "Tell me more about that counselor position."

"I have to be interviewed for it."

"No way." I try to look interested, but I'm really wishing she'd go to the bathroom or something so I can lift the lid on that leftover pizza and handle my business.

She twirls her braids. "I have to come up with something I can teach the younger girls at camp. I think I'll teach them soccer. Plus Ms. Worthy, she's on the counselor selection committee, is coming to spend a day with me."

I rest my head in my hand with my elbow on the table. "Why is she coming?"

"She visits all of the nominated camp counselors and assistants. She wants to meet our families and hang out with us for a day, just to see if we actually use what we learn at camp."

I nod, just to let her know I'm listening. But all the while, I'm enjoying just sitting with her, listening to her go on and on about MVP stuff. I love how it feels talking to a girl. It feels awesome to buy her something to eat and share it, even though I sneezed all over it.

Sergio and Tasha pass by our table holding hands. Makeda waves, but neither Sergio nor Tasha waves back. Sergio scans Makeda from head to toe, then shakes his head. Is he trying to compare honeys? Maybe Makeda isn't as fine as Tasha, but at least she's not stuck up like spit wads on a ceiling.

Makeda's still talking and I smile. She smiles back before taking a sip of her Coke. Right now, all I want to do is make up for all the rotten things I've ever done to her. I can do that, because it's time to move the L-Train on down the railroad tracks of love.

I hope you're ready, Makeda, because I'm going to pop the question.

# Chapter Seven

$I$'ve got a big glob of *duh* stuck in my throat. This is the most important moment of my life, and Wally Wimp, the word-grabbing imp, is swinging on my tonsils.

"Lamar, are you okay?" asks Makeda.

"Uh-huh, yeah, I'm good."

I scoot closer to the table. What's wrong with my palms? I wipe the sweat on my pants. Is it hot in here? My stomach gurgles. Maybe the pizza was bad. Makeda tilts her head at me.

"Are you sure?"

"Uh-huh."

Just ask her, fool! Alls she can say is "No and

go away" or "Get out of my face." I've been told that before. What's the big deal? I swallow hard and the chump glob disappears.

"Makeda, have you do a boyfriend?"

"What?"

Dang. What the heck did I just say?

"Uh, what I meant to ask is, you kickin' it with anybody?"

She tugs at the ends of her braids and grins at the table. "No."

"I don't have a girlfriend either."

She doesn't respond. I'm sure it's because she's thinking how lucky she is that the L-Train is still available. She checks her watch.

"I have to get home, Lamar. Dad and I are going to the basketball game tonight."

My watch shows two thirty. We've been talking for two whole hours. She gets up and wipes the pizza crust crumbs from her skirt. I'm not ready to say good-bye.

"Can I walk you home? I mean, I'm going to the game and was planning to leave soon too."

"Okay."

I'm wheezing and don't care. "Did you say okay? I'll turn in my bowling shoes and be right back."

I put my shoes on the counter, take a quick puff of my inhaler, and join her at the door. We walk out together. I've never walked out of Striker's with a girl. Besides Mom.

On our way to her house, we see more posters announcing that Bubba is coming to Coffin. I tell her about how much I've learned from his book and she listens. She talks more about soccer and MVP camp. I can hear the excitement in her voice. Now she's got me curious.

"So when will you know if you got the job?"

"I don't know. I've never been nominated before."

"Talk about pressure. I sure hope you get it, Makeda. I bet the girls will love playing soccer."

"Have you ever played?"

I show her my inhaler. "I don't have the lungs for it."

"Oh. Too bad, because it's a lot of fun, but it's almost constant running except for maybe the goalie. I practice every day. I'd rather play soccer than eat."

"I feel the same way about bowling. So besides soccer and bowling, what other things do you like to do?"

She looks to the clouds. "Reading, baking—oh, and I love poetry."

She turns toward a house on the corner. An elderly woman is rocking in a chair on the porch. She waves at us and I wave back.

"Who's that?"

"My grandma. Just keep waving. She's a little senile."

My arm's getting tired, but Grandma's hand keeps flapping in the wind. Makeda blushes and shrugs.

"Maybe I'll see you at the game."

"Yeah, that would be tight."

She's smiling and my palms feel clammy again, my weight shifts from one leg to the other, and my brain is empty, like it's been wiped clean with idiot soap.

I press my lips together. "Makeda, I was wondering . . ."

Her front door opens and a man as big as Shaq steps out. I take two steps away from Makeda. She introduces us.

"Daddy, this is Lamar."

I step closer and give him a firm handshake. "Nice to meet you, Mr. Phillips."

"Likewise, Lamar. Aren't you Xavier Washington's brother?"

"Yes, sir."

"He's one heck of a ball player. You shoot hoops?"

"No, sir."

"Football?"

"No, sir."

"Soccer?"

"No, sir, but I *am* the King of Striker's."

"*Hmm*. Yeah, that brother of yours, he's going to put Coffin on the map one day. Tell him I said good luck tonight."

He hugs Makeda and I shoot for the good impression.

"I'll give Xavier the message, Mr. Phillips. It was great meeting you."

I get my strut working. People stare, but I don't care. That's right, move out of my way. I just walked a girl home and met her daddy. A terrible thought pushes through and steals my thunder.

Wait a minute.

I slow down to a complete stop and sit on the curb near the soccer fields with my elbows on my knees and my hands cupping my face. Mr. Phillips thinks I'm a chump. He didn't even comment on my bowling title. I bet he doesn't even think bowling is a real sport. He thinks I'm a loser and he might make Makeda stay away from me.

I have to do *something*. I've never gotten this close to having a girlfriend and I don't want to blow it. Maybe I could try out for soccer. That'd make Makeda and Shaq Daddy happy.

My hands slide from my face to my lap as I sit up and give this more thought. Makeda said goalies don't run that much. I could be a goalie. And maybe Dad would come to my games.

I stand and step back onto the sidewalk. This plan is getting better by the minute.

A clear visual of Dad, Makeda, and Shaq Daddy sitting together on the soccer field bleachers excites me. I'd block a couple of scoring attempts by the other team and be the hero. Yeah, then Dad would hurdle the bleachers, storm the field, and lift me high in the air as I raise one finger in victory.

I better get with Dr. Avery. Maybe he's got some extra-strength medicine for guys like me. I've got twenty minutes before Dad leaves for Xavier's game. Avery's office is down the street and over a few blocks. I pick up my pace and go for it.

Minutes later I'm at the doctor's office. Hanging from his door is an old rusty sign that used to say WELCOME. But it lost the *c* and the *o*, and now it just says WEL ME.

I do an extra round of breathing exercises before going in, just for good luck. I turn the knob, and a cowbell *doodle-ling*s like in some old country store. The place is crammed with women knitting or reading, crying babies, and crawling toddlers.

Trina, Dr. Avery's receptionist, greets me with a toothy grin.

"Hey there, Lamar. Where's your dad?"

"Oh, he's at work."

"How's your brother?"

"Fine."

"There's a game tonight, isn't there?"

"Yes, ma'am."

"Well, tell Xavier that I said good luck. You're not scheduled for an appointment today, are you?"

Time out. She's got an appointment book in front of her and can't remember if I have one, but she can remember Xavier has a game. I keep my cool.

"No, ma'am. I need to make an appointment, you know, just a follow-up."

Trina takes a look at the appointment book. "You're in luck. This is Dr. Avery's Saturday in the office. I've got an afternoon opening tomorrow at one o'clock. You want it?"

"Yes, ma'am, I'll take it. Oh, my dad won't be with me this time. But he said it's okay, because I'm old enough to see Dr. Avery on my own."

She writes my name in the scheduler. "Just be sure to have your dad call me, okay?"

"Oh, uh, sure. I'll have him call."

"Good. See you later. I may see you at the basketball game tonight."

I give her my best sophisticated expression. "I'll be there, but I'd really rather be at Striker's. Have you ever tried bowling? It's way better than hoops. You should check it out."

She smiles. "Dr. Avery says the same thing. I'll keep that in mind."

"Bubba Sanders, the baddest bowler in the universe, is coming to Striker's on the Fourth of July. That would be a great day to come."

Trina tilts her head. "I've seen the posters. Maybe I will."

I wave and strut out of the office. I feel slicker than worm spit. If I can get Avery to say yes to soccer, then I'll try out for a team.

I better put a move on it. After jogging two blocks, I begin to wheeze, so I stop and take a puff from my inhaler. Dad's going to be mad if I'm late. For him, missing a tip-off is one degree worse than burning the house down. This game decides the championship bracket. If X's team wins, they're in.

I hope they lose by a hundred points and it's all Xavier's fault.

## Chapter Eight

I turn the corner and notice Dad is in the car with the motor running. I rush to the back door and open it.

"Sorry, Dad."

"Lamar, you know I hate to be late to your brother's games."

He punches the accelerator, speeding through back alleys and other shortcuts to save time. Once we arrive, Dad and I rush to the gymnasium door.

It's sauna hot inside the gym. The funky blend of sweat and armpits fills my nostrils. Fans stand shoulder to shoulder and root for their team seemingly unbothered—it's as if I'm the only person who can smell that.

Athletic shoes screech as players race up and down the floor, pointing and shouting out instructions. I glance at the scoreboard. Xavier's team leads by six points. I climb to the very top of the bleachers, where the air might smell and feel different.

Standing up and sitting down, up and down, the crowd can't make up its mind what it wants to do. I stay seated because I really don't care. As the crowd stands again, Makeda pops into my thoughts. She looks good in there, walking around in my mind. Wow, she's blowing me kisses. What'd you say, Sweetness? Yeah, I love you, too, girl. What? Of course you can have another kiss from the L-Train. My eyebrows jump with each mental conversation until my pocket buzzes.

At first, I think it's some mutant insect that's crawled up my pants leg. I stand while everyone else is seated. Then I remember my cell phone. I take it from my pocket, flip it open, and press Talk.

"Hello?"

"Hey, Washington, I'm near the gym doors. Let's take a walk. I'm dying of boredom. You down?"

"Sure, why not. I'll meet you at the concession stand."

I tromp down the bleachers and cut my eyes

toward Dad. He's too preoccupied with the game to notice I'm on the move. Billy bumps fists with me, and we stroll down the long halls of the Y.

He tries a few doorknobs, but they're all locked. He stops in front of a tinted door.

"Ah, the computer room. Dude, I love computers, especially laptops. The Y just got six new Dells." He turns to me. "You can take classes here. Did you know that?"

I nod. Billy cups his hands to the window and keeps talking.

"You can see out, but people can't see in. I love that."

I want to ask him why he's trying to see in if he knows he can't, but I don't. We move farther down the hall and make a right turn.

"Check it out, Washington."

He stops in front of a fire alarm in the middle of the hall. He caresses it, and I'm starting to feel uneasy. Billy talks without taking his eyes off the alarm.

"Ever pulled one of these babies?"

I'm scared to move. "Nope."

He runs one finger over the word FIRE on the alarm. "It's a megarush out of this world. My dad made me crazy mad one time and I pulled the alarm at his job. People scattered like roaches. It was the ultimate prank. They never figured out who did it. If you ever want to get someone back, pull one of these. It totally rocks."

I nod and step away. Billy joins me.

"Xavier the Basketball Savior is a sweet nickname."

"It's a'ight I guess."

"Scooter and my dad think X will get drafted, maybe straight out of high school."

I stuff my hands into my pocket. "Your brother's pretty good, too, Billy. Xavier says Scooter's the best center on the team."

"Scooter's okay, but not as good as X. Even if your brother doesn't get drafted, he'll get a full ride to some major college. How about you, Washington? You going to college?"

I shrug. "I don't know. Maybe, if I can get a bowling scholarship."

Billy laughs. "You're joking, right?"

"Uh, no."

Billy opens an exit door and I follow him outside, where he pulls a pack of cigarettes from his pocket and extends them to me.

"Want one?"

I take a step back. "No. I have asthma."

"Oh, then I won't light up. You know, having money in your pocket opens up a world of opportunity for you, Washington. I mean, what if that bowling scholarship thing doesn't happen? You can make your own scholarship, know what I'm saying? Pay your own way through school. And how about new gear? Or you can buy Christmas gifts for your dad and something nice on Mother's Day for your mom."

"My mom's dead."

Billy stares at me. "No way. My mom's dead, too. That's crazy weird."

He searches the grass and opens up about life with his mom. I talk about mine and he listens.

"If Mom were still here, tomorrow morning, actually every Saturday, I'd get banana pancakes for breakfast soaked with hot maple syrup. You ever had syrup on your bacon?"

Billy nods. "Heck yeah, that's good stuff."

I stare at the grass and relive thousands of things I could tell him about her. Fun and food, hugs and help, smiles and tears revisit my memory to give me options. I tell Billy as much as I can without getting all emotional.

"She sounds pretty awesome," he says.

I don't look up. "She was way cool."

Billy snatches a handful of grass out of the ground. "I don't think anybody really understands guys like us. How can they? Take Sergio, for example. He gets everything handed to him on a silver platter."

"Sergio's cool, Billy. He's my best friend."

"Hey, nothing wrong with that. I'm just saying, with Mom gone, I became a man a lot faster than some of these rich kids. I know I'm making my mom proud, taking care of myself the way I do. I bet your mom is proud, too, Washington."

I can barely hear Billy. I'm still enjoying the mental motion picture of times I spent with Mom curled up on the couch watching episodes of crime shows. Sometimes she even joined me to watch bowling tournaments that Bubba bowled in.

"Earth to Washington."

I look up and smile. "My bad."

Billy gives a half grin. "No apology necessary. I get lost in my thoughts all the time. I understand. I really do. Listen, I've got a match set up at Striker's tomorrow at noon. It's a small bet. We won't make enough money to buy a rally towel, but it's good practice. I want to get this smoke in before the game is over. See you later."

Billy walks around the corner to the back of the building. I smell cigarette smoke and move farther away. Maybe I've been wrong about this guy. I've only heard rumors about his drama. I've never seen him in juvie, boot camp, or under arrest. It could all be a pack of lies.

People get labeled for stuff. Maybe that's

what's happened to Billy. Or maybe he's changed; Makeda's a perfect example. She's changed. I think I have too.

Since my girl likes poetry, I'm going to write her an unforgettable poem. I've got all kinds of talent, and I want her to understand I'm not just a bowling stud with a handsome face.

Cheers erupt from inside the Y and I sprint back to the gym. Ten seconds left and the game is tied. Xavier calls time-out. It's standing room only on Coffin's side. I rush to the visiting team's bleachers and sit with the Bedford fans.

The buzzer sounds, the bleachers rattle, and the noise levels are out of control. X dribbles over the half-court line. Fans stomp to raise the noise level. This is it. Winner plays in next Wednesday's championship game; loser buys a ticket and watches with the rest of us.

Coffin fans chant X's nickname as if they're casting an evil spell.

*"Xavier, Xavier, the Basketball Savior! Xavier, Xavier, the Basketball Savior!"*

Dad chants, too. Mr. Jenks screams and points at Scooter. Hundreds of Bedford fans lead a charge of their own.

"Dee-fense!" *Clap-clap!* "Dee-fense!" *Clap-clap!*

Between my teeth I chant with the Bedford fans and tap my foot when they clap.

Xavier passes the ball to Scooter, then dashes to the left corner. A Bedford player tries to keep up with X. Rubber soles screech on the court as picks are set, cuts are made, and players scramble to beat the buzzer. Five seconds, four . . .

Scooter screams something to Xavier and throws the ball to a spot near the three-point line. Xavier spins away from his defender and catches the ball before it bounces. The Bedford player rushes to catch up, but it's too late. Three, two . . .

Xavier leaps high in the air, higher than his defender, and releases the ball off his fingertips toward the basket. Mouths close, eyes bulge, fans freeze. It's eerily quiet as the ball arcs and spins in the air. One . . .

*Swish!*

*BEEEEEEEEEP!*

Dad jumps off the bleachers and beats the coach to Xavier. He lifts X in the air, making my brother resemble one of those gold dudes on his trophies at home. My heart hurts as I rewind my thoughts to earlier in the day when I daydreamed about Dad lifting me up in the exact same way.

Coffin fans rush the court. Bedford fans clog the exit.

A man with a microphone stands at midcourt to announce Coffin as the team that will play Scottsburg for the Indiana YMCA championship next Wednesday. Then it gets worse.

"Attention, please! The committee has posted the All-Y team, and we're proud to announce Coffin's own Scooter Jenks and Xavier Washington as First Team All-Y members. And, no surprise to most of us, Xavier has been named MVP of the game."

It's time to go. It doesn't matter how long they celebrate on the court. I'm not celebrating. If I have to, I'll stand at the car and wait all night.

## Chapter Nine

**I** sit on the front bumper of Dad's car, content to chill until he and X come out of the Y. My legs feel funny. I stand to stretch and drop face-first in the grass. My legs tingle and tickle at the same time. I'm sprawled out like a chalk outline at a murder scene when Makeda appears. She giggles and holds out her hand.

"Need some help?"

I take the offer. "Either my legs fell asleep or this is what happens when you're bored to death. You heading back to Striker's?"

I purposely don't let go of her. She doesn't try to pull free, so I keep holding on and she blushes.

"I was on my way over to sit with you, but you left with Billy."

Dang. "Yeah, we were just bored, that's all."

Her dad calls her. She smiles at me. "I've got to go. Bye, Lamar."

She slides her hand out of mine and sashays away. I'm not ready for her to leave, so I scramble for something to say.

"I'll have something for you tomorrow."

She turns to me and walks backward. "I'm helping my grandma wash her clothes tomorrow. It'll be after one before I get to Striker's. What do you have for me?"

"It's a surprise. You'll see. You're going to love it. And anyway, I've got a doctor's appointment at one, so two is cool, okay?"

"Okay."

Soon, Makeda and her dad drive off. Twenty minutes later, I'm sitting on the lone car left in the parking lot when X and Dad come out. They're laughing and talking about that unbelievably lucky buzzer beater X threw up in the air. Dad unlocks the car with his remote and I take the backseat. As Dad starts the car, he catches my eye in his rearview mirror.

"Wasn't that an awesome game, Lamar?"

"Awesome."

"Your brother wants a big fat juicy steak, and I

think he deserves one, don't you?"

"Yes, Dad, he deserves it," I say while thinking about my girl.

At the Wabash Steak and Seafood House, Xavier orders the biggest and most expensive steak on the menu. Dad joins him. I order catfish and think about Sergio. Dad yanks a pen out of his shirt pocket and clicks it several times, then pulls his napkin closer.

"Okay, X, look at this. When Coach calls for the one-three-one offense, he wants you to feed your big dog in the middle. Hit Scooter with a soft lob and he'll roll right to the bucket for an easy two. Then when you get the urge to pop a three from the top of the key, he'll set a pick on your guy strong enough to hold back Niagara Falls."

I get an idea. "Hey Dad, got another pen on you?"

He finds one and gives it to me. I grab my napkin and go to work while he and X are going back and forth on strategy. After a while I notice that their conversation has stopped. I break off a piece of catfish with my fingers and toss it in my mouth. Dad grins.

"How's your fish?"

"Crunchy. Hey, can you think of anything that rhymes with *Makeda*?"

"Wow, that's a tough one. Not offhand. Did you

do your breathing exercises today?"

"Yes, sir. I also stopped by Dr. Avery's office and made an appointment for tomorrow. Will you call and tell them it's okay for you to *not* be there?"

Dad raises an eyebrow. "I can be there. What time? Is something wrong?"

"No, sir, nothing. I'm thirteen now and it's just going to be the same old 'Breathe in, breathe out' routine. You know Dr. Avery never flips the script."

Dad winks at me. "I get it. You're almost a man now. Can handle your own business."

Xavier opens his big mouth. "You should take him, Dad. Lamar's a baby. His breath still smells like Gerber."

"Shut up, X! Dad, it's time. You're absolutely right. I'm old enough."

He reaches into his wallet and hands me a twenty. "This is for the insurance co-pay. I'll call tomorrow and give my consent."

I stuff the cash in my pocket. "Thanks, Dad. Did I tell you I've beat Sergio in eleven straight games of bowling?"

Dad chuckles. "No kidding?"

"He can't handle me, Dad. I'm the bowling king at Striker's."

He nods as he chews, then gets this oh-I-meant-to-tell-you look on his face.

"I did some research on that bowling

scholarship thing we were talking about a few days ago. Nada. Zilch. Couldn't find one school willing to fork over a bowling scholarship. I guess things haven't changed."

If Xavier's grin gets any bigger, his head's going to explode.

I scoop a big chunk of potato salad into my mouth. Then, out of nowhere, Dad taps on the table.

"You know, bowling on a team is one of my happiest high school memories."

I stop chewing. So does X. Dad's eyeballs bounce back and forth between us.

That's just as good as pulling the clip on a grenade and dropping it in on Xavier's head. My mouth opens. Potato salad falls out and splats on my plate. Did I hear what I think I heard?

"Did you say you bowled on a team?"

His head tilts. "I told you that, didn't I?"

Dad keeps chewing and reloads his mouth with steak. "*Mm-hmm.* Yep, I was nasty good. Bowled cleanup, you know, anchor. My teammates called me Clutch. Clutch Washington. I won a trophy. It's somewhere in the closet at home."

I've got clumps of drooled potato salad on top of my catfish. I drape my napkin across my plate. The catfish was good, but not nearly as good as this bit of news.

"I knew you bowled, but I thought it was just for fun," I say.

He gobbles more steak. "Boy, I loved to bowl as much as you do now. It's too bad they don't have bowling teams in schools anymore."

"Yeah, that would be way cool. I'd roll lights out for my school."

Dad chuckles again. Xavier tries to break in, but I'm not having it.

"Hey Dad, when you find that trophy, I want to see it."

"Really? Okay, I'll look for it. Anything exciting happening at Striker's?"

I quickly glance at Xavier. He thinks the conversation is over, but it's not.

"Bubba Sanders is coming on the Fourth of July."

Dad's fork stops halfway between his plate and his mouth. "Is he really?"

"And he's giving away four of his brand-new Pro Thunders with the matching bags."

Xavier breaks in. "What's he going to do, chuck the bowling balls out in the crowd and whoever doesn't get knocked out gets to keep 'em?"

Dad laughs at that one but then gets serious. "Really, what's the catch?"

"You have to write a five-hundred-word essay to Bubba by June thirtieth, explaining why you should be one of the four lucky winners."

Dad's eyebrows rise, "*Oooh*. That's brutal. Have you finished your essay? You *did* enter the contest, didn't you?"

I've got enough money in my Bank of Lamar to buy half of a Pro Thunder right now. But that information is top secret.

"I haven't entered it yet. I hate essays. I may have to pass on this."

Dad wipes his mouth. "I don't know, Lamar. You aced every essay you wrote in school this year. Winning should be a cakewalk for you. Plus, it's Bubba Sanders!"

I give Dad a high five. "I know, right?"

There's a goofy grin spreading across my face. It feels awesome. For the first time ever, I think Dad understands me.

"So Dad, just how good were you on the lanes?"

He pokes another piece of steak. "How good? Try a two-oh-two average. Imagine that. After all these years I can still remember."

Xavier laughs and points at me, "Even if you tried out for some bumper bowling squad, you'll never top Dad's old scores. I can't believe Mom thought you'd ever be a superstar. Super*loser* maybe. Now *there's* a trophy that already has your name on it."

I point my fork at him. "Leave Mom out of this!

And Dad was talking to me."

Dad holds up a hand. "Hey, hey, okay, settle down, you two."

X rolls his eyes and restarts another basketball conversation with Dad. My brain flips the switch, too. I work on my girl's poem.

What rhymes with *Makeda*?

# Chapter Ten

*E*arly Saturday morning I crank through my chores like a walking energy drink. I take extra time for my breathing exercises. Standing in front of the mirror, I breathe in through my nose, out through my mouth. My lungs need to sound excellent today.

When Dr. Avery puts that stethoscope on my chest, he needs to hear nothing. No wheezing, no weird stuff. In through my nose, out through my mouth. I check my watch: eleven o'clock. I've got two whole hours to roll a game or two at Striker's before my appointment.

I make a quick sandwich and burn off. It's

perfect weather outside today. That's got to be a sign. It's going to be a *yes* day for me. I feel it.

Once inside the bowling alley, I head straight to the snack bar. There's Sergio. Tasha's not with him. Being the man that I am, I strut over to my boy.

"What's up, Sergio."

He shrugs. "Nothing much, just waiting for Tasha to get back."

"Where'd she go?"

"To some fashion store. I gave her thirty bucks to buy a pair of jeans she saw in the window."

I smile at him. "Sergio, the way you give that girl money should be against the law."

He raises a brow. "Don't worry about what I give my girl. You need to worry about what your girl is giving you."

"What do you mean?"

"She's ruining your rep. Don't you get it? People are going to talk about you and Fivehead. Aw, man, you're on your way to a really bad crash and burn."

Something has just crashed and burned all right, and it may have been our friendship. I'm tired of him talking bad about Makeda when his girl's middle name is ATM.

"Tasha's not perfect, Sergio. And today, I'm going to ask Makeda to be my girl. If you don't like it, too bad. And don't call her Fivehead when you're around me."

"I'm just trying to help you out, Lamar. I told you what girls look for in a guy. I didn't know I needed to tell you what guys look for in a girl."

I bang the table. "You're supposed to be my best friend. You should be happy I've got a honey. Thanks for the support, Sergio."

The conversation freezes. Sergio takes a sip of his drink, and I take a puff of my inhaler. I bob and sway to the song playing through the speakers. Finally, he holds out his fist to me.

"You're right, bro. I won't say anything else about her. Let's not talk about our girls anymore. Let's just flip the switch on that conversation, okay?"

I scoot closer to the table and we bump fists. Sergio leans back in his chair. Something's still bothering him. It's all over his face. So I call him out.

"Spill it, Sergio. What now?"

"I want to talk to you about something."

"I'm listening."

"About those gutter balls yesterday."

I cross my arms and tilt my head. "What about 'em? It wasn't my fault."

"And I guess you're going to tell me you didn't know Billy was going to throw 'em?"

I tap the table with my fingers. "Billy was try-ing something new with his game."

"Come on, Lamar. It's bad enough that you're hanging with Billy. What's next?"

I lean back hard in my chair. "What's up with you, Sergio? If you don't want to hang out with me, just say it! But all this extra drama . . . I'm just not down, bro."

Sergio won't look at me. But he won't say those friend-killing words either. So I let him off the hook.

"Have you finished your essay for Bubba?"

His head snaps back to face me. "Almost."

I search my brain for conversation. "What's going on with the Holiday World trip?"

Sergio leans in. "You mean you're still plan-ning on going with me?"

"Why wouldn't I? I'm pumped about hanging out, just you and me and the fattest wooden roller coaster on the planet."

He nods and smiles. "Now you sound like Lamar. Maybe we can leave after Xavier's game. Dad's going to hang out with an old college friend who doesn't live far from the park. They'll drop us off early. Then we can be first in line Wednesday morning and stay all day."

"If I could skip X's game and go straight to

Holiday World, I would."

My cell phone buzzes and I take it out of my pocket. Sergio leans to look.

"When did you get that?"

"Yesterday."

"Did your dad buy it for you?"

"No. Hey, I've got to take this call. Later, Sergio."

"Where are you going?"

I wave him off and stroll toward the empty video games area before pressing Talk.

"Hello?"

"Hey, Washington, I'm down on lane thirty-six. I've got two guys visiting from Kentucky who think they've got game. I've already paid for both of us. Get your ball and shoes. It's time to go to work."

"Dude, where do you find these people? Did you say they're from Kentucky?"

"When it comes to money, people find each other. Word gets around just like my business card. I met Jesse Ray in boot camp. Others like Omar and Sandeep, I made the hookup at school, okay? Now get down here!"

Boot-camp bowlers? My brain is throwin' gutter balls. I try to bail.

"Listen, I've got a doctor's appointment in an hour."

"I told you about this yesterday at the Y. We

can't back out. If you've got a doctor's appointment, then you better get down here and take care of business."

The phone dies and I take off for lane thirty-six. I pass Sergio again and he's still asking questions.

"Where are you going?"

"I'm going to bowl a game with Billy, that's all."

He crosses his arms. "He's playing you."

We lock eyes. I don't answer. I don't have time.

I pick up the pace and enter the bowlers' area. Billy introduces the two high school guys from Lexington. I do a quick scan of them for guns and knives. I watch their every move. The game starts and I do what I do, but these country boys don't act like boot campers. I can't picture them locked up for doing anything wrong. I get so relaxed that I give them a few pointers.

"Find the book *Bowling with Bubba* and study it. It'll change your game."

Billy pushes me. "Don't give 'em your secrets, Washington! Geez!"

After Billy and I send those guys back to their old Kentucky home, we divvy up in the men's room.

"It's a light day. Only twenty bucks each, but that's twenty bucks closer to getting that Pro Thunder, right?"

I slide the twenty into my pocket. "Did you

meet those guys in boot camp?"

Billy nods. "They got fingered for stealing car radios. Do they look like thieves to you? Bad raps are common in boot camp. You'd be surprised, Washington."

I shrug. "Yeah, I guess so."

He opens the door. "I'll be in touch."

I'm late for my appointment with Dr. Avery. I can't make a bad impression on my first visit without Dad. Besides, this is no ordinary visit. I need a favor from Dr. Avery.

A big favor.

## Chapter Eleven

**M**om must have been desperate when she hired Dr. Avery. She said he specialized in children's respiratory problems. I think he's full of crackers and cream cheese. I wheeze just as much now as I did at four years old when he first diagnosed me with asthma.

Later, in kindergarten, Dr. Avery made me a child chump when he wrote a "Lamar can't play" note. My teacher read it to me and then sentenced me to the library during recess. That same note made me a certified member of the nerd herd on the bleachers during gym class. Worst of all, I got labeled a "no-pick" for everything, and the title stuck as I grew.

I knot up every time he says, "No, Lamar, you can't play that sport" or "No, Lamar, you can't run that race." Each *no* comes with the same routine. He pushes his glasses up the bridge of his nose and sips whatever he has in his Styrofoam cup. One day I asked him.

"What's in the cup, Dr. Avery?"

"Coffee," he said.

I think it's Haterade.

I push the door and tolerate the stares as the country cowbell *doodle-ling*s. I sign in and give the receptionist the copay money. She says Dad called her and she'll have my receipt ready when I leave. I look for a regular seat, but they're all taken. The receptionist points to the right.

"There're probably a few seats around the corner in the children's play area."

It's been ten years since I've sat around the corner. I barely remember what it looks like. When I turn the corner and scan the room, memories race back.

"Ouch!"

I plunk my head with my knees when I bend to sit on a four-inch-high safari animal chair. Two snotty-nosed rug rats want to rub my "booboo."

"I'm a'ight," I tell them.

My knuckles rest on the carpet. Is that a baby blue rhino in a pink tutu dangling from the ceiling? Please, just hurry up and call my name.

A door creaks open around the corner.

"Lamar Washington?"

I roll out of my chair and shoot my two new rug rat friends a peace sign.

Nurse Sharon greets me at the door. "Good to see you, kiddo. Doing okay?" she asks.

"I'm doing great—actually, fantastic."

She looks over her shoulder at me.

"Take a seat in room four. Dr. Avery will be with you soon."

He always listens to my lungs, so I unbutton my shirt. A knock on the door and a slow turn of the knob alerts me. He pokes his head in before fully opening the door.

"Hello, hello, how are you doing, Lamar?"

I mimic him. "Good, good. I'm doing real good, Dr. Avery."

He sits on his stool, puts his Styrofoam cup on the counter, and grabs my chart.

"Well, you're obviously not here for a sick visit. How can I help you?"

"I want to play soccer. Do you have a stash of supermeds, you know, something that might help me if I decide to try out?"

He keeps reading my chart. "I didn't know you

liked soccer, Lamar. I thought you were a bowler. Best game ever."

"You're right about that. This soccer thing is just temporary. But I'm going to need something stronger than my inhaler if I try out. I know you've got something that'll help me."

I pull a twenty from my pocket, tuck it in his lab coat, and wink.

"And here's a little extra something for your trouble."

Dr. Avery takes a quick sip from his cup and flips the page in my chart.

"You're not trying to bribe me, are you, Lamar?"

I just smile. Of course I'm trying to bribe you, fool!

Dr. Avery resembles a black Albert Einstein, except his nappy gray afro reminds me of a sheep's butt. And his fro has a hole in the middle where he's going bald. If he had a flag on top of his head, you could practice golf putts.

He puts the stethoscope plugs in his ears. "Let's take a listen."

I breathe big breaths for him.

"When was the last time you used your inhaler?" he asks.

"About an hour ago."

"You sound great, Lamar."

I keep breathing big air. "I've been doing

my exercises every day."

"Good, good, very good."

After I suck all the good air out of the room, he pats me on the shoulder.

"Well, your lungs sound clear, but I'm afraid not clear enough for soccer. Your allergies can flare at any time, especially in the soccer-field grass. Unfortunately I don't have any miracle drugs for you. And in good conscience, I must advise you to stay clear of soccer, especially knowing how quickly your air passages can narrow. I'm sorry."

"Are you telling me I can't even try out? There's got to be something at the drugstore. Just write a prescription for a few pills, not a lot. I just want to make the team."

"I'm sorry, Lamar, but—"

"Wait, stop, didn't you hear me? I probably won't even get in the game."

He pushes his glasses up the slope of his nose and picks up his cup.

"You have the worst case of asthma I've ever seen. You've been hospitalized six times with life-threatening asthma attacks. Your lungs are still very fragile, Lamar, and I'm not willing to jeopardize your life for a silly game of soccer."

"Soccer isn't silly, Dr. Avery. Maybe you just can't figure out the game, just like you can't figure out how to help me."

He puts his hand on my shoulder. "I under-stand you, Lamar. Three years ago when you sat on this very table and told me you wanted to play sports, I recommended bowling. And from what I hear, you're one of the top young bowlers in Coffin. Do you still bowl with your dad?"

"Not really."

I can't stop my mind from flipping calendar pages, way back three years ago when Mom took me to Striker's for the first time. We bowled with bumpers, laughed, and ate junk food all day. Eventually, we graduated from bumpers to regu-lar bowling, even wore matching blue T-shirts, as if we were a team. Saturdays belonged to Mom and me.

After she died, Dad took me to Striker's a few times, but then he fell off. Our fun dropped to none. It seemed like he could only remember how to get to Xavier's games.

I clench my teeth, shrug, and squint at Dr. Avery. "You can't dribble a bowling ball, and there's no hoop at the end of the bowling lane."

I frown at the perfect lungs on a colorful poster of the human body taped to the wall. As I stare at the poster, I feel Dr. Avery's eyes on me. He lets go of my shoulder.

"I'm sorry, Lamar. I wish I could help more."

"Me too."

I hop off the table and don't bother to button my shirt before leaving. The receptionist holds out a receipt, but I don't take it.

"Okay, no problem, I'll put it in the mail," she yells.

It's hot outside, but not nearly as hot as I am right now. I come out of my shirt and tie the sleeves around my waist. Dad doesn't like me walking around outside in a muscle shirt and saggy jeans. He calls that look ghetto and thuggish. But I don't care today.

I cut a sharp left down Eighteenth Street. I need to bowl. I need to hit something. Halfway to Striker's, I detour down an alley and kick the base of a Dumpster. There's no one around, so I look up to the sky and take it out on God.

"It's not fair! Why did you give me bad lungs! Why can't I be normal? You made X normal! Why didn't you take him instead of Mom? Our house is all messed up now."

I lean against the Dumpster and slide to the ground. Tears fall without permission. It's not like I hadn't known what Dr. Avery might say. But I wanted it so bad. A *yes* and a few superpills would change how people see me. I wouldn't seem so wimpy to Dad or even Mr. Phillips. But there's nothing I can do. I get up, wipe my eyes, and stuff my hands in my pockets—and that's when it hits me.

Dr. Avery kept my money.

He's lucky that twenty wasn't my only one, or I'd go back and snatch it out of his lab coat. Plus I'm in the parking lot of Striker's and I don't feel like going back to his busted office.

I open the door to Striker's. The air conditioner cools me off in more ways than one. I'm happy to be away from the doctor's office and back in the land of teenagers, bowling lanes, and hip-hop music. No safari chairs or tutu-wearing rhinos in here.

"Lamar!"

Makeda floats toward me, looking dynamite in her blue soccer uniform.

"How did the doctor's appointment go?"

"As usual. You feel like taking a walk? I do."

"Okay. Let me tell my friends I'm leaving and get my bag."

When she returns, I take the bag off her shoulder. "I'll carry this."

We're barely out of Striker's parking lot when she starts bugging me about the surprise.

"Come on, Lamar, tell me what it is."

"Not yet," I say.

I catch her looking in my hands, trying to get a clue. As we pass the Little League football and soccer fields, I stop and turn to her.

"I wrote you a poem."

Her expression makes me happy that I took the time to do it. She scurries to a tree near the chain-link fence surrounding the soccer fields and takes a seat in the grass. I slow strut toward her to add drama to my presentation, making her giggle.

After taking her bag off my shoulder, I pull my masterpiece from the back of my jeans and unfold it.

"You know, it was hard finding words that rhyme with *Makeda*."

She shrugs. "Yeah, I bet that was tough."

"And this took me a while. . . ."

She frowns. "So are you going to read it or what?"

"I'm going to read it—just let me finish what I want to say. I worked really hard to put into words what was on my mind."

She rolls her eyes. "Lamar . . . today already."

I clear my throat. "Okay, here goes.

*"Makeda, Makeda,*
*You fine sweet potata*
*Sugar and spice*
*Is what you are made a*
*MVP camp is where you should go*
*But first, will you be my girlfriend*
*Yes or no?"*

I raise my eyes from the paper and wait for her to tell me it's the best thing she's ever heard, but she doesn't. She's not even looking at me. I go sit next to her under the tree.

"What's wrong? You hated it?"

She nods. "I liked it a lot. And I'd really like to be your girlfriend."

"Then why won't you say yes?"

"What if you decide to go back to being the old Lamar; the one who puts tacks in my chair and high-fives my forehead? I'm scared of that. I mean, how stupid will I look, kickin' it with a guy who clowns me? That would really hurt my feelings."

Dang. I should have worked harder on that poem. Maybe I should have made something rhyme with *I won't make fun of you anymore*. I take her hand.

"Makeda, you gotta trust me. I don't know what else to do, but please, don't tell me no. Come on, give me a chance."

We sit under the tree in silence for what feels like six months, and watch cars and people go by. It's two fifty. I've done all of the begging I'm going to do. I'm not moving until this girl gives me an answer. She tugs my T-shirt. I cut my eyes to her and brace for my second rejection of the day. Instead she nods.

"Okay. My answer is yes."

"For real?"

"For real, Lamar."

"Okay, okay, cool."

I scramble to my feet and offer her my hand. She takes it and I help her up. We stare at each other like we're aliens from the planet Dense. She giggles and shrugs.

"So, what now?"

I shift my weight to the other leg. "Maybe we should seal the deal."

She stares at the sidewalk but I can see a smile on her face. "How?"

"I don't know. Maybe we should bust a slobber or something."

Makeda's eyes widen. "My dad can see this far. If he catches us kissing, trust me, you can't run fast enough."

I look for the perfect spot. There's a hole in the links of the fence leading to the back of the soccer bleachers. I know these bleachers pretty well from all the times I've come to watch Sergio play Little League football. I get closer to examine the area, then motion to her.

"Come on, follow me. Stay low and quiet."

I go through first and hold the links apart so she won't snag her clothes. We go deep under the bleachers to the very end, away from the sun peeping through.

"How's this?" I whisper.

"Perfect."

I take her hand. "Okay, ready?"

"I think so."

I lick my lips and move toward her face. Light shines behind her from the spaces in between the long seats. I lean toward her and she closes her eyes. I close mine, too, and keep leaning closer and closer.

Okay, maybe I've never played a sport in this place. But in a few seconds, I'm going to . . .

Score.

*Mmmm.*

We pull away at the same time.

"Your lips smell like strawberries and taste like 'em, too," I say.

"It's my lip gloss. I got it free when I bought two facial cleansers and hand soap from Mom's Mary Kay lady. I've got more flavors at home. I've got cherry, peach . . ."

I kiss her again because I'm not trying to hear about Mary Kay. This time when I pull away she stays quiet, so I lead her back through the fence and onto the street. Once we hit the sidewalk, I release her hand so I won't catch a beat-down from her father.

Talking seems wrong for this moment. So we just stroll in silence. She turns onto the patch of sidewalk that leads to her porch. I wave at Grandma.

Makeda takes a few steps forward and stumbles, then looks over her shoulder at me and giggles. I know why. The L-Train knocked her off her track! She's love drunk from these luscious lips of passion! I kick my strut into fifth gear. Holy guacamole! I've got a girlfriend. I lift my top lip closer to my nose and take a big whiff. *Mmmm.* I love strawberries.

## Chapter Twelve

It's four o'clock and I'm in front of our house. This has to be the earliest I've gotten home all summer. I'm licking Makeda's strawberry lip gloss off my mouth like it's leftover pork chop grease.

There's a poster on a stick stuck in the ground near our porch steps. Once I'm close enough to read it, my eyes burn.

Xavier Washington
1st Team All-YMCA
Summer Basketball MVP

I've got some MV pee. I look around. Nobody. I unzip. Just as I'm about to add a yellow smiley face, Dad opens the door and peers over the porch. Dang.

"What do you think of the sign?"

I zip up and nod. "Nice, it's really nice, Dad."

"A couple guys at work helped me make it. Not too shabby for a homemade job, don't you think? Hey, how'd the appointment go with Dr. Avery?"

"Fine, but I'm ready for an adult doctor."

Dad chuckles. "That's fair." He buttons his uniform shirt as he comes down the steps. "I forgot I switched shifts with a friend today. I'm working five P to five A. Tell your brother about my shift change, okay? See you in the morning."

I plop on the couch and turn on ESPN. Bubba's bowling. How did I forget about this? Just as I get comfortable, I hear the front door open.

"Where's Dad?"

I don't turn around. "At work. He switched with somebody."

"He's supposed to help me with algebra. The final exam is coming up. I have to pass!"

He clenches a basketball between his hands and shouts at the ceiling. I watch his meltdown until it's Bubba's turn to bowl. X steps in front of the television with his basketball tucked under one arm. He snatches the remote from my hand.

"I can't study with all of this noise in the house," he says.

"Fine, turn the sound down. You've got the remote."

"It's not the television. Get out, Lamar. I need the house to myself."

"Hey! It's not my fault Dad bailed on you."

I stand and try to see around him. He gives me a hard push and I fall back on the couch. Ever since Mom died, it doesn't take much to set him off. Like when he bombs a test or misses a game winner or doesn't understand something. X goes dead red and I know to stay out of his path. Dad took him to see some anger management shrink. Xavier has medication, but I don't think he takes it.

He comes toward me. "You think you're special, with your perfect grades, don't you?"

I shake my head until I'm dizzy. "No. There's nothing special about me."

"But what do you have to show for it, superstar? Mom's note?"

"You're right, X. I'll just go to my room until you cool off."

I'm wheezing, but I know he doesn't care. I try to leave. X cuts me off.

"See, what you don't understand is I don't need all of this school stuff. I'm going pro after high school. Have you heard about the scouts coming to the championship game? They're coming to see *me*! But if I don't pass algebra, it's over. No varsity ball, no pro ball, no nothing. College isn't for everybody. Kobe Bryant didn't go. LeBron James didn't go."

I try to walk by him again, but he gets all up on me.

"You've got five minutes to get out, Sleazy Wheezy. I'm calling my girlfriend to come over, and I don't want you here."

"I thought you were going to study."

"So did I."

His eyebrows rise. He bites his lip and cuts his eyes to his algebra book on the table. But seconds later, he's back on my case.

"Tonight, I'm switching from algebra to anatomy, know what I mean? So get out. You've got four minutes. I'm not playing."

He pushes me again. I scramble to the door.

"Okay, I'm leaving."

I slam the door and stomp down the steps. After a quick swoosh from my inhaler, I kick the base of X's poster. It leans to the side. If some of the neighbors weren't out, I'd finish my mellow-yellow project.

I bet Sergio's watching Bubba. It's a ten-minute walk from my street to his subdivision. Two-story mansions with four-car garages, long circular driveways, and landscaped lawns are all you see. Sergio lives on a big corner lot in a gray stucco house. He opens the tall wooden door.

"What do you want?"

"Are you watching Bubba? I came over to watch him with you."

He moves to the side to let me in and I explain. "I was watching him, too, but X told me to burn off."

"For what? Hanging out with Billy?" Sergio asks.

I glare at him. "No."

We walk toward the living room. There's a sheet of stamps and a box of envelopes on the table next to a flyer about Bubba coming. I stare at it until Sergio moves to face me.

"Dude, it's not too late. You could still do an essay. As much as you love Bubba, it's almost your duty to write one."

I keep staring at the stamps. "You already mailed yours?"

"Mailed it this morning."

I snap out of it. "Good for you, Sergio. But I'm still not writing one."

He frowns. "I guess bowling with a guy who fakes gutter balls to cheat people out of money is easier for you than writing an essay."

I stop in front of the sofa. "Why are you sweatin' me?"

He crosses his arms. "You're ruining everything."

"Like what?"

"Your reputation, for starters."

I roll my eyes. "You don't know what you're talking about."

Sergio steps closer. "Billy's a thug, Lamar. You know it, I know it, and the whole town of Coffin knows it. You let him put shame in your game. All your talk about bowling and Bubba. You totally disgraced both of 'em."

"What's it to you, Sergio? I'm doing what I want to do. Can't you understand that?"

I try to sit down, but Sergio puts his hand on my shoulder and spins me back to face him.

"You're the best bowler I know, Lamar. But your brain is in sideways, fool. You're not the King of Striker's anymore. You're more like the King of Hustlers."

I step toward the front door and put my hands to my head. "I'm not trying to hear this every time I hang out with you. I'm handling my business and I don't know why you can't see that." I turn back and point at him. "I mean, if you were handling *your* business, you'd know that Tasha just likes you for your money. She's a gold digger with cheddar and you don't even see it."

Sergio's on my heels. "I thought we weren't going to talk about our girls anymore."

I get outside and turn around. "Okay, okay, I went out of bounds. My bad, Sergio."

He nods. "Forget it. Come back inside. I won't say another word about you and Billy. Let's just watch Bubba cream somebody's corn."

I take a step toward his door. My phone buzzes. Sergio looks at my pocket and then back in my face. I answer the call in front of him.

"Hello? Yeah. Twenty minutes? Can't you change it to later? Okay, I'm on my way."

I snap my phone and drop it in my pocket. "I gotta go."

Sergio steps back inside. "Whatever."

## Chapter Thirteen

Inside Striker's, I look for Billy. The crowd is thin and the music isn't thumping like it usually is. Striker's seems different, or maybe it's me. I hear someone whistle. It's Billy.

"What's going on, Washington?"

"Hey, Billy. What lane are we on?"

"It got cancelled. One of the dudes got an emergency call from his dad to get his butt home. It was too late to call you back, so I thought maybe we could just hang out or something."

Unbelievable. If Sergio walked in right now, our friendship would die forever. Heck, it might already be dead. My weight shifts to one leg.

"You should have called me anyway. Bubba's rolling. I was just about to watch him mash somebody's potatoes. I rushed here for nothin'."

"My bad, partner. From now on, I'll call you if somebody backs out."

He points to a table. "Check it out. Two pepperoni pizzas with extra cheese and a pitcher of Coke on the table just for us. And since there's nobody playing on lane thirteen, the manager's showing Bubba's tournament. See, you haven't missed a thing."

I shrug. "Okay, I guess. Let's eat."

We stroll to the table. I pour myself a glass of Coke and tear away a piece of hot pizza. Billy pulls out a chair, turns it backward, and sits with his chin resting on the high part. He grabs a slice and drops half of it into his mouth. As I eat, drink, and watch Bubba, my conversation with Sergio replays over and over again. I look over at the empty table where he usually sits with Tasha. Dang. I'll call him later. Billy taps on the table, pulling me out of my thoughts.

"You weren't with Makeda, were you?"

I think about what I want to tell him. I decide to leave Sergio out of the mix.

"I was at home, but X is trying to study."

Billy slurps his Coke. "And he can't study while you're there? Are you *that* noisy?"

I stop chewing. "It's not even about the noise. He's just crazy."

"You seem a little edgy, Washington. What's going on?"

"Nothing."

Billy scoots closer to the table. "Hey, we're partners, remember? We share everything. It's okay—I won't tell anybody."

I grind my pizza with tight jaws, mashing the cheese and pepperoni as I think about what X did to me.

"It's my brother, that's all."

I stare at my Coke, but I feel Billy deadeyeing me. He puts his hands on the table and leans in. "Can I tell you something? I mean, it's like nonrepeatable."

I look up. "I'm listening."

"I get knocked around by Scooter, but who's going to believe me? He's Mr. All-American, and this town would drink his bathwater if he'd let 'em. So I take his beat-downs. Only guys like us understand what it's like living with a jock. You'd be surprised how many guys I talk to about this very thing, Washington. There's a bunch of us. Sometimes, I come here at night and bowl a few games, just to get my head on straight."

We both grab another slice of pizza. He's gobbling his and I'm tripping on what he just said. Is there a secret underground society of abused and misused younger brothers? I thought I was alone. I don't know if I feel better or worse knowing this. Does X know? He probably does. That's why he pounds on me and expects me to take it.

We knock off one pizza. Billy closes the box and tosses it on the floor.

"Be honest, Washington. Does X do stuff like that to you?"

I tell Billy everything. It's the first time I've opened up and talked about the beat-downs I take from my brother. All the times he rats on me to Dad, calls me "superstar" like it's a bad word, or just picks on me for no reason. I tell Billy how X pushes me around and how I'm sick of it.

"You know, it's amazing how many things we have in common, Washington."

I wipe my mouth. "Yeah, I know. It's almost scary."

Billy counts on his fingers. "You needed cash flow, so did I. Your mom's dead, so is mine. You've got home problems, me too."

I shrug. "So what?"

Billy turns his chair around and sits the right way. "I don't think it's a coincidence. You need help with a situation, and I've got the absolute perfect advice for you."

I stop eating. "What?"

Billy leans in. His icy blue eyes freeze me. The left corner of his mouth turns upward and I zone in to hear every word.

"Don't let X push you around. Trust me—nobody's going to believe you. Actually your situation is worse than mine because your brother is straight golden, know what I mean?"

"Yeah, I do."

"If X goes crazy again, hit him where it hurts the most."

I look at my lap. "You mean . . ."

"No. I mean basketball. He loves hoops more than anything. Mess with his game and he'll get the message. Do something ridiculous, cause a scene, try to embarrass him. Remember what I told you about pulling the fire alarm at my dad's job? It totally worked."

"What can I do to embarrass X?"

"That's for you to figure out. But the next time he picks on you, plan a disaster party with him as the special guest. It doesn't matter if he finds out who did it. The idea isn't whether or not you get caught; the point is to get even."

"Yeah, maybe I will."

"No maybes, Washington. Be committed. If he goes off, you go off. Understand?"

"Yeah, Billy, I got it."

He chugs the rest of his Coke and grabs the

last piece of his pizza.

"Call me if you need help with your plan. Unwind, Washington. Finish your pizza. Bowl a few games. See you around."

I take Billy's advice. I take the pizza and pitcher of Coke to a table behind a lane and roll until I feel better. There's one piece of pizza left, so I eat it as I walk home. I think about everything Billy said. With every step toward home, I get stronger in my commitment.

It's dark outside when I ease in the house. X turns over on the couch and restarts his snore. An algebra book lies open on the coffee table. I don't smell any girly perfume, so I figure he probably spent the evening alone.

I tiptoe to my room and close the door. The last thing I want to do is wake up my brother. He'll be fighting mad if I startle him. I'm not in the mood to get punked tonight. But I do know one thing. When Xavier goes off on me again, thanks to Billy, it will be the last time.

## Chapter Fourteen

Sunday afternoon, right after church, Dad takes X and me out for lunch. Two platters of appetizers later, Dad complains about being sleepy. He drives home and both he and X fall asleep. Too many buffalo wings, fried cheese, and potato wedges. I keep my church clothes on and pay a visit to my girl. She's never seen me pimped out like this—light blue collared shirt and dark blue khakis. I want to look nice, since I might meet her mom.

I'm a few steps from turning on the patch of sidewalk that leads to her house when my cell vibrates. No way. Not now. I turn my back to the house and flip open the phone.

"Yeah, Billy?"

"I think I've got a monster gig lined up. Meet me at Striker's in five minutes."

"But I'm busy right now. Give me an hour and I'll be there."

"Did you hear what I said? This is business, Washington. Be here in five."

The phone goes silent. I flip it closed and shove it into my pocket. Bump Billy. I'm going to spend some time with my girl, and he'll see me when he sees me.

Makeda's grandma sits on the porch with a bowl in her lap. She gives me a huge, toothless grin, and I feel the buffalo wings from lunch take flight in my belly.

"What's your name?" she asks.

"Lamar."

She holds out her bowl. It's full of peanuts. "Would you like some? Go ahead and grab a handful."

I really don't want any, but to be nice, I take a handful and stuff them in my mouth. Man, these peanuts are off the chain! They're sweet and salty and remind me of Mom's snack mix.

She holds the bowl up. "Take some more, baby. Aren't they good?"

All I can do is nod, because I've got a serious

chew rhythm going on. The door opens. Makeda has an apron around her waist. I swallow the peanuts and smile.

"You cook, too? I love pork chops. You know how to fry pork chops?"

I dig into Grandma's bowl and scoop another handful. I chuck the nuts in my mouth and crunch them down to peanut butter. Makeda wipes her hands on her apron.

"I didn't know you were— What are you eating?"

She looks at her grandma's bowl and then at me. I'm chomping away, bobbing my head to my own crunchy beat.

Makeda gently touches her grandma's shoulder. "Grandma, we'll be right back."

She takes my hand and leads me inside her house. I'm nervous about holding her hand and look for her dad to pop out from behind the curtain or something. I'm scoping the place for him when the door shuts behind me. I spin around. Makeda's frowning.

"Are you eating peanuts from Grandma's bowl?"

I nod because I've got a mouth full of them.

"Didn't I tell you she was senile?"

I nod again.

"Those peanuts used to be chocolate covered. Grandma sucks the chocolate off, then spits the nuts back in that bowl. We try to stop her, but she keeps doing it. How many have you eaten?"

My jaws lock. My tonsils lift to the roof of my mouth just to get out of the way. There's a shift happening in my belly. Something's rushing toward my throat. I press my hand over my mouth. Peanut goo seeps through my lips and spreads between my fingers. Makeda points to their bathroom.

"Ugh, you better hurry, Lamar."

My wicked brain flashes pictures of Makeda's toothless grandma grinning at me. No doubt about it. This is going to be violent.

I make it to the bathroom, face the toilet, and lift the seat. I can't believe I've got my face hanging low, staring at blue water inside someone else's—

*Nuuuuuuuuoooooooaaaaah!*

I'm embarrassed by the high and low barf noises. Oh no, that was peanuts and Buffalo wings. I hurl until nothing comes up but echoes from a hollow belly. At the sink, I scrub my hands and wipe my face to erase any signs of peanut goo.

There's a bottle of mouthwash on the counter, so I unscrew the cap and gargle some, just to rinse my inners. When I open the bathroom door, Makeda and her parents stare at me.

"You must be Lamar," says Mrs. Phillips.

I nod in case my breath blows fire from leftover barf juice.

Makeda and her mom talk at once. Mr. Phillips

grins. Makeda steps toward me.

"Are you okay?"

I silently belch a minty taste from the mouth-wash. "I'm much better now."

Mrs. Phillips apologizes. "We just can't seem to pry that bowl away from her. We weren't expecting company today."

Mr. Phillips shuffles toward the television and parks on the couch. Makeda moves toward the door. She seems excited.

"Ms. Worthy is coming Tuesday morning."

My eyes widen. "The lady from MVP camp?"

Mrs. Phillips smiles at me. I'm so happy I paid attention. Makeda nods.

"I'm making chocolate chip cookies for her."

"Won't the cookies be hard by Tuesday?"

"I'm just making the dough. I'll freeze it and then bake the cookies early Tuesday morning before she gets here. They'll be delicious. So I'm a little busy right now."

It takes a minute, but I get the hint. "Oh yeah. Good luck. I'll see you later."

I look beyond Makeda to the living room. Her dad is still grinning. I bet he stocks chocolate-covered peanuts for Grandma just to keep dudes away from his daughter.

Makeda opens the door. "I'll walk you to the street."

We pass Grandma on the porch and she holds out her peanut bowl. I want to knock it out of her hand. But instead, I do what Mom would want me to do.

"No, thank you. I've had plenty. See you later."

As we reach the sidewalk, I look down the street.

"I was hoping we could take another tour of the soccer bleachers."

She giggles. "Is that all you think about? I'm so excited about Ms. Worthy coming. This is the biggest thing that's ever happened to me."

I nod. "Don't worry. You've got that gig locked up."

My phone buzzes. I'm ready to throw it in the sewer.

"I gotta bounce." I wink at her. "See you later."

I flip open my phone and walk at the same time.

"I'm on my way."

Billy screams into my phone. "Dude, where are you? You better not blow this deal for me. Get to Striker's now! I can't talk about it over the telephone."

"I'm not far away. Hang on."

Three minutes later, I walk into Striker's. The place is crowded with old people. It's the Sunday-afternoon Seniors League. It smells like sore-muscle ointment in here.

Billy paces near the snack bar. He wipes his forehead and grips his bowling bag.

"We've got the biggest bet ever lined up in Wabash. Our ride's outside."

I don't budge. "Wait, back up, Billy. I've got to let my dad know where I'm going. And why is this game in Wabash?"

"It's rich preppies. They insisted we play on their turf. I agreed. The bet is two hundred bucks per person, Washington. Did you hear me?"

I need another fifty bucks bad. I lost twenty to Dr. Avery and another twenty on pizza and drinks for me and Makeda a few days ago.

Maybe Dad won't miss me for an hour or so. Billy walks and I follow him. There's a cab waiting. We get in. The driver turns around and glares at us.

"Where to?"

"Wabash Bowling Lanes."

"Young man, that's going to cost you forty bucks. Are you sure?"

Billy tosses two twenties onto the front seat. "I'll give you another ten if you hurry."

The gears shift and our driver burns off. If Dad finds out that I left Coffin without his permission, the tires on this taxi won't be the only thing burning.

## Chapter Fifteen

I slump in my seat to hide. Our driver is NASCAR crazy, weaving through traffic, pressing on the horn and cursing other drivers who won't move out of his way. All for ten extra bucks. We're going to die.

Billy talks on the phone, assuring our competitors we're on our way. He's pleading with them as if they're ready to call it off.

Soon we pull up in front of Wabash Bowling Lanes. Billy drops another ten-spot on the front seat and jumps out before the cab comes to a complete stop. He hollers and points at me.

"Hey driver, give my friend your business card.

We'll call you when we're ready."

I get the card and catch up with Billy inside. Before I can say anything, I'm totally freaked by the ugliness of this place. The lights are dim and the place is a ghost town.

I bet Wabash Bowling Lanes doubles as Wabash Funeral Home. It's eerily quiet in here, no music playing, dingy red carpet without any colorful swirls in it like at Striker's. Dang. I'm dying just standing here. And it's Sunday! This place should be packed.

"Washington, we need to talk."

"What's up?"

We walk toward the video games, and he puts his arm on my shoulder.

"I need you to gutter your first two rolls, okay?"

I slam my brakes. "What? No way."

"I'm going to double our money. I'll make these guys think you blow and then sucker them into doubling the bet. They're rich boys."

My brain searches for answers. "We're undefeated. We can beat them."

"Just listen to me. Then, in the third frame, I want you to switch back to bowling lights out, okay? Just follow my lead, Washington. I know what I'm doing."

This reminds me of a football coach asking the worst player on the team to take a cheap shot on the opposing team's quarterback. I'm a flunky, a hired chump. On top of that, I'm wheezing.

After I take a quick puff from my inhaler, Billy pats me on the back.

"You a'ight? Handle your business and you'll have enough for that ball you want."

Somebody whistles. Two guys signal to Billy. He looks their way and points.

"I see 'em, down near the low lanes."

I squint. "Is that hair on their faces? They look old enough to be in college."

Billy nods. "They are. Keep walking, we're already late."

"What? You set up a game against college guys and you want me to fake the funk? Are you out of your mind?"

"Relax, Washington, and get your head on straight. This is not the time to chump out. Don't worry about them; focus on your game. I'll take care of everything else."

I slow my pace. "Billy, even if we win, these guys might take our money, knock us around, and then make us walk home. I can't believe I came all the way out here to get jacked up."

He jerks around to face me. I've never seen this look.

"This game is mega, understand? I've been waiting all summer for a payday opportunity like this. I want you to drop those gutter balls like hot grease, and then bowl lights out. Got it? Now man up. It's time to go to work."

I don't like Billy's tone. That's mighty big talk from a guy short enough to be the mayor of Munchkinland. I understand he's nervous. And we *are* partners. And I guess there's a lot of money at stake. Okay, I'll handle my business, but after this game, Billy's going to hear from me. And if he tries to chump-talk me again, I'll crush his cookies.

Billy enters the bowlers' area. "Thanks for waiting, guys. Hey, nice shirts! Which one of you owns the red corvette? Actually, the Lexus convertible must be yours? Yeah, that's what I thought."

I block out Billy's butt-kissing session and give these college boys a once-over. There must be lots of money in Wabash. These college chumps make sure we see their Rolex watches and diamond stud earrings.

One has on a white designer shirt with the collar popped. I laugh at his played-out look.

I check out the ball return and roll my eyes. This is where they should have spent their money. Instead, two cheap no-name bowling balls sit side by side on the ball return like butt cheeks. Mr. Popped Collar nods my way but speaks to Billy.

"Is he your partner? Where's his gear?"

Billy turns to me like I'm new in the place. I speak for myself.

"Uh, where's the shoe rental booth?"

Both guys laugh so loud it echoes off the walls. Mr. Popped Collar points down the carpet.

"If you're bowling in house shoes, you need to go that way. What a joke."

The other guy joins in. "Just bowl in your Jordans. Who cares?"

I can still hear them raggin' me as I step up to the rental booth. A teenager wearing a yellow polo shirt with WBL stitched on the pocket comes to the counter.

"Welcome to Wabash Bowling Lanes. Do you need rental shoes?"

"How much are they?"

"A dollar and fifty-four cents. That includes tax because everything's half off on Sundays."

I give him money for a size nine. He gives me an ugly pair of two-tone bowling shoes and keeps one of my Jordans. If the shoes are this grubby, I can't even imagine how terrible the balls must be. I find a rack of twelve-pounders and can't believe my eyes.

Three green Bubba Sanders Pro Thunders sit on the rack. They sparkle with a newness that excites me. I want to tell someone what I've found, but I don't think they'll care. I wonder if this is where Billy got his. I stick my fingers in the holes of the first one.

*Awwww. Ooooooh.* I'm bowling with this baby.

As soon as I return, Billy takes a look at my ball and grins. I set it on the ball return. These guys don't seem fazed by the presence of greatness. Mr. Popped Collar steps forward with four one-hundred-dollar bills in his hand.

"Billy, show me your money. Two bills per bowler. No backing out and no excuses. Are we doing this?"

Just before he answers, the front door of the bowling alley flies open and bangs the back wall. The biggest man I've ever seen, bigger than Makeda's dad, makes a path down the carpet. At least twelve feet tall, this fee-fi-fo-fum dude stomps our way in a dingy T-shirt, blue jean shorts, and army boots. My heart thumps "Taps," because no one in my family knows I'm here and I bet this dude is a chainsaw killer.

Judging by the looks on our competitors' faces, they don't know Goliath either. But Billy does.

"Hey, Uncle Mickey, thanks for coming over on such short notice."

Billy strolls over and gives the big guy a hug. Holy guacamole, the giant is on our side! My chest puffs out. Leave it to Billy to find an equalizer.

"Washington, come over here and meet my

uncle Mickey. He's going to hold our money until the game is over."

I pimp my walk, sporting Wabash Bowling Lanes' house shoes. Billy introduces us. As I head back to my seat in the bowlers' area, Popped Collar whispers to me.

"House ball and house shoes. What a joke."

I stand next to the Pro Thunder on the ball return.

"This isn't just an ordinary house ball. This is a Bubba Sanders Pro Thunder. I can't believe there're three of them collecting dust on the racks. That's crazy."

Popped Collar shrugs. "It's just a ball. Nothing special about it. Never heard of this Bubba guy either. But he sounds like a big country hillbilly to me."

He just won himself a chin check. I ball my fists. Nobody talks about Bubba like that. Billy yanks me away.

"Pump your brakes, Washington. Like I told you before, everybody's not down with Bubba. Use that anger. When it's time, introduce them to the King of Striker's. Don't forget the plan."

I look over my shoulder at Uncle Mickey, then at Billy. "I'll be back in a second."

My strut is hard with purpose and soul. I've got to set things right and get this place ready for a Coffin-to-grave experience. At the shoe rental counter I ring the bell for service. The teenager seems bothered that I'm back.

"Yes?"

"You got a radio or something?"

"We try to keep the noise down in here, since the balls and pins make such a racket."

"Not today." I point at Uncle Mickey. "He likes hip-hop and he wants it on right now. Or you can tell him what you just told me."

The teenager shrugs and walks to the back. "No problem, I'll turn it on."

I lean over the counter. "And he's hard of hearing, so thump it!"

Seconds later, a beat breaks off in the speakers. The bass guitar rumbles through me and a rapper talks trash about his skills. The guy working the snack bar bobs his head and puts popcorn in the popper. It's time to get this party started.

I lock in on everything Bubba says in his book. First, I take a seat and prepare myself to bowl. Second, I check the lanes. They're oily, which means my ball is going to slide a lot before it actually begins to roll. I need to adjust for that.

Third, cancel everybody, even Billy. This isn't about money. This is about Bubba.

Billy tries to introduce me to the rich boys.

"Washington, this is—"

I cut him off. "I don't want to know. I'll just call them Pete and Repeat. Put me last."

Billy shrugs at the preppies. "Whatever."

There's nothing but squawk and gobble coming from those starched-collared turkeys. I'm strolling to my seat when Popped Collar tries to punk me.

"Don't take this beating personally, House Shoes—may we call you House Shoes?"

I raise one eyebrow. "Whatever, Pete. Or are you Repeat? It doesn't matter."

Dang. How am I supposed to talk trash when I'm sending my first two rolls down the lazy river? This better work or I'll never be able to show my face here again.

Billy rolls first. He spares, and that's good since he usually has a slow start. Pete strikes and Repeat spares. I give Pete a long look. He's mine. I take my ball from the return and stand on the lane. Billy yells mixed messages.

"Come on, Washington. Roll us a strike."

I hold the ball close, take four steps, swing it back, and aim for the gutter.

*Thump!*

My ball waddles toward a mass of blackness next to the pins.

"Dang, it slipped," I say.

Billy goes ballistic. "I thought you told me you were good?"

Pete and Repeat hoot. I can't look at them. I can't look at Billy either. Once my ball returns, I grab it, stand the same way, take the same walk, and throw that same ball.

*Thump!*

Billy bangs on the scorer's table. "We are so dead, Washington."

"It slipped off my fingers again. My bad. I'm going to get a different ball."

Popped Collar hollers to me. "I told you to leave those Bubba balls alone."

I step up to the rack and grab the next Pro Thunder in line. This isn't about the money anymore. I'm going to crush their cookies.

When I come back, Billy whispers that those chumps have upped the bet.

"One more gutter frame, Lamar. Then follow my lead."

I sit and wait. When it's my turn, I throw another bad one. Pete and Repeat laugh.

Billy walks up to the lane. "Lamar, calm down. Just relax and try to hit your mark. Come on, we're going to lose if you don't get with it!"

I roll a ball close to my mark and knock down four pins. Billy claps. I turn and grin at him. I really want to grin at Pete and Repeat because their party's over. I'm about to open up a can of Wabash on them and they don't even know it.

When it's my turn again, I get up and make an adjustment to my normal roll by moving my feet just a little to the right on the approach line. *Focus, Lamar.* With Bubba's Pro Thunder resting on my side, I feel power oozing from the ball. Here comes something stank filthy. I just know it.

*POW!*

Billy fist-bumps me. I don't look at the preppies on my way back to my chair. I don't have to. They stop bumping their gums, and that tells me a lot. That's right, I got skills.

Billy gets hot. His third frame is a strike. Pete and Repeat argue over whose idea it was to bet so much money. Pete throws a split. Repeat gets a spare.

It's my turn again. Pete leans forward in his chair.

"What would that Bubba guy say if he knew you were bowling gutters with his ball and wearing house shoes?"

My heart sinks for a moment. Am I disgracing Bubba in front of these haters? No. No way. And I'm going to prove it by making them respect Bubba's ball, my skills, even these busted house shoes. I look over my shoulder at Pete.

"I'll show you what he would say."

I take my time, find my mark, and roll a nasty message down the wood.

*BLAM!*

Popped Collar fakes a clap. "Lucky shot."

With a smooth move, I snatch my comb from the back pocket of my church pants, fluff my fro, and pimp-walk back to my seat. Pete and Repeat watch me. For fun, I stop in front of them and pretend to wipe something off my rental shoes.

I roll so many *boom*s, *blam*s, and *pow*s on them that by the ninth frame, we're so far ahead, Billy calls our cab driver. In the tenth, I roll three more exclamation points to be high scorer at an even 196. Billy stands in the bowlers' area like it's no big deal.

Pete and Repeat congratulate me on a great comeback. They want to shake hands, but I'm not down. It's not that I'm a sore loser, but to me, it's just not that kind of party. They talked trash about Bubba.

I kick off the rental shoes. My feet and toes expand back to normal. Repeat tries to smile at me.

"Hey, Washington, nice game. What's your secret?"

I hold up the house shoes. "These."

I stand next to Uncle Mickey and break those boys off. "In Coffin, we call the spanking you just took 'punked, skunked, and slam-dunked.'"

I turn to my partner. "I'm out."

"Sure, Washington. Our cab's on the way. I'll be there in a minute."

I want to scream like the pro athletes do when they pull off something spectacular. I want to spray paint KING OF STRIKER'S WAS HERE on their rides.

I'm outside airboxing, throwing jabs and hooks, bobbing and weaving, feeling untouchable. Billy shuffles out with his uncle Mickey. The big guy waves and drives away in an old truck just as our cab pulls up. Billy drops forty bucks on the front seat for the driver, then gives me four crisp one-hundred-dollar bills.

"You rock, Washington! I can't believe how you totally humiliated them! This is the best payday I've had all summer. You've made enough money in three days to buy your own Pro Thunder. Three days! Essays are for Siss-ays, know what I mean? Next time I'll triple our bet."

I stare at my open hand with four large bills sitting in it. I've got enough money right now to buy two Pro Thunders, and that doesn't include what's in my Bank of Lamar at home. Billy's right. I'll put cash on the counter, baby, just like a real man. I'm at the top of my game and no one can handle me.

Billy and I relive the entire game while riding in the cab. I'm laughing and watching signs on billboards as we ride by. One particular billboard catches my eyes and drops four hundred dollars' worth of guilt in my lap.

## SERGIO'S AUTOMOTIVE REPAIR SHOP
### HONEST WORK. HONEST PRICE.

Billy's still bumping his gums about the game, but I've mentally checked out of that conversation. What have I done? What the heck am I doing? Pete was right. How would Bubba feel if he knew I faked the funk? And before I can dog myself for bringing shame to my game, Sergio's angry face visits my conscience and tells me what I already know.

*You cheated.*

## Chapter Sixteen

*E*arly Monday morning I sit on my bed and make myself a promise. No more cheating. I don't care what Billy says. I cross my heart and move on because I've got money to count.

All my money is spread across the bed. I need a drumroll.

One hundred, two hundred, three hundred, four hundred, four hundred and fifty, sixty, sixty-five, sixty-six, sixty-seven, sixty-eight dollars and forty-four, forty-five, forty-six cents! Holy guacamole—$468.46! I stuff the $8.46 in my pocket; $460.00 is a nice round number. I put the top on my bank and place it back in my closet.

I rush to my computer and pull up several different websites for bowling equipment. One store in town has Bubba's Pro Thunders on sale for $205.00. Yes! Yes! I dance around the room and congratulate myself for being the man. I did it!

Mom would be so proud of me. Maybe not for the gutter balls, but overall, she'd give me a thumbs-up. I sit on my bed and think about her. Birds chirping outside bring me back from deep thoughts.

I need to get to the lanes. This may be the last day I bowl with a house ball. There should be a way I can mark this moment as another part of my dud-to-stud transformation. Bump that. I'm out. Two blocks from Striker's, I see my boy strolling down the street. Okay, I can do this. Don't mention anything about yesterday.

"Yo, Sergio!"

He stops and waits for me. "Are you heading to Striker's?"

I nod. "Heck yeah, it's two-for-one hot dog day. I'll walk with you."

Sergio checks his watch. "I'm meeting Tasha. Don't forget Bubba's rolling this afternoon. It's that big tournament in Arizona. He won it last year."

I pretend the sidewalk is a bowling lane and roll an imaginary ball.

"He bowled straight gas last year. One of his games was a two-ninety-eight, two pins away from a perfect game—it was so awesome. The tournament starts at five right?"

"Yep, and I've already told Tasha I'm leaving early."

I open the door to Striker's. "I'm leaving early, too. So if you don't see me, that's what's up."

I love Mondays at Striker's. It's never wall-to-wall crowded. Hot dogs are two for the price of one, and I purposely skip breakfast because those dogs are barking good.

Sergio and I walk in. Tasha strolls over, ignores me as usual, and takes all of my boy's attention. I get my two dogs, rental shoes, and ball because I don't want to talk to her anyway. I'm way down on lane thirty-eight. There's no one on the left or right of me.

This is perfect. I just want to roll alone. I deserve a private celebration for what I've accomplished. Today, I don't want my cell phone to buzz. I don't want Sergio and Tasha bugging me. Makeda's my girl, but today, I want to roll solo.

I do crazy stuff like bowl between my legs and bowl backward. I try curve balls and even bowl with my left hand. When I'm through, I head to the snack bar and order a big plate of French fries.

Sergio and Tasha are three tables away, but I can hear Tasha the Tick sucking more blood out of my boy.

"Just twenty dollars, Sergio. Come on, I really want these earrings."

I purposely push my napkin off the counter. As I reach to get it, I see Sergio snap a crisp twenty out of his wallet. He glances over his shoulder, and I make sure he sees me watching him. Tasha gives Sergio a peck on the cheek and leaves. I wipe my mouth with my wrist, eat the last two fries, and leave him sitting there too.

"Later, Sergio. Don't forget Bubba's rolling at five."

He nods but doesn't say anything. If I could shake some sense into my boy, I would. Sometimes he just refuses to see the truth. Some things I just can't talk to him about.

My watch shows four thirty. I rush into the house and make two salami sandwiches and a glass of chocolate milk, then move to the living room. ESPN is showing highlights of yesterday's baseball games.

I settle in and take a bite of my sandwich when X stands in front of the television with his hands behind his back. His flaring nose and fiery eyes put me on red alert.

"What do you want, X?"

"Dad's working another double shift. He wants you to fix us dinner."

I don't want any trouble, so I slide him my other sandwich.

"Here."

X brings his right hand from behind his back. "I don't want your stupid sandwich. I just want you to see *this*. Look what Dad found."

It's a bowling trophy. I reach for it, but he keeps it from my grasp. I don't know if I'm excited to see it or sad that I won't be the first Washington to showcase a bowling award. X points to the mantel.

"It needs to go up there."

I take another bite of my sandwich. "Then move one of your trophies to make room."

I chug my chocolate milk but watch X pace like a restless caged panther. His steps are silent. I'm scared to move. I've seen his anger before, but he's never been like this. So I try to slow his roll.

"Okay. You're right. Dad's trophy needs to go up there. Maybe you can take one of yours down and give Dad some space. Oh, I know, then Dad can have a bowling trophy up there and when I get mine, I can take Mom's note down and put my trophy up."

By the look on his face, my idea was not the one he had in mind. Actually, he seems angrier than before. So I come right out and ask him what's up.

"You got a problem, X?"

"What's *your* problem, Lamar? Dad's into basketball. He's into me. You think you and Dad are going to have some bowling bond, some trophy tie? No. I'm not moving any of my trophies. The note needs to come down now."

"It says 'Reserved for Lamar's first trophy.' Not Dad's, not yours."

He keeps pacing. "The only way a bowling trophy makes this mantel is if I stick Dad's up there. Get real. You're never going to bring home the hardware."

I put my sandwich down. "Shut up, X—that's not true."

He stops in front of Mom's note. "When Mom tacked that yellow Post-it for you, I'm sure she believed you'd have *something* up there by now."

My face warms and I stand in front of the couch. "Shut up!"

"Aren't you embarrassed by that? I can't believe she tagged you as the superstar of this family. You're a total disgrace to her memory."

I can't take it. "I said shut up! That's between me and her. Just give Dad one of *your* stupid spaces."

"No way. My trophies deserve to be up there. Dad's trophy deserves to be up there."

He stops in front of Mom's note. Our eyes lock.

He's dead red. I'm code blue.

"Please, don't do it, X."

His arm reaches up and I dash toward the mantel, but I'm a step too late.

*"No, don't!"*

*R-r-rip.*

I lunge and knock him to the floor. My sandwich flies, my glass rolls. Dad's trophy falls from Xavier's hand.

With both fists, I pound him over and over again. "I hate you!"

He grabs my arms and flips me. My head bangs the floor. His fists pound my face, shoulders, chest, and stomach. One solid blow connects with my chin. I taste blood oozing from inside my mouth. Soon, the only fists flying are his. And he talks to me with each brutal blow.

"I hate you, too, Lamar. No matter how many trophies I put on that mantel, it was never enough for Mom. You were her favorite. But guess what? You're not getting Dad."

I close my eyes and take the worst beat-down of my life. Please, just let me pass out. Maybe if he hits me enough, I'll go be with Mom. But he stops, crumples Mom's note, and throws it at my chest.

"If it means that much to you, post it in your room. But this mantel's for real champions."

He steps over me, opens the front door, and slams it closed. I reach for Dad's trophy. It hurts to move. I manage to stand and place it above the fireplace where Mom's note used to be.

It's their mantel now, not mine.

I swallow the blood puddle in my jaw and stagger to my room. Mom's note is in my balled hand. I uncurl my fingers.

Oh God. It's bad. I rush to my bed and place the note next to me. I try to straighten out what X did. But I can't. It's crumpled and wounded. One edge is torn. I place it on my lap.

It's weak and sick just like Mom was when she died. I close my eyes and wish I hadn't. I beg the memory to stop. *No, please don't take me back to the funeral.* But it's too late.

The pews are packed. Our red-and-white-robed choir sings "Amazing Grace" as I slump in the front row at Second Baptist Church in a black suit I swore I'd never wear again. I hate that suit and that song. Dad's crying. Xavier covers his face. I'm not crying. I'm begging Mom to get up. But she doesn't. So I stare at my black shoes just so I won't look at her casket.

A quick shake of my head snaps me back. I force my eyes to open. Tears race down my face. I press the note against my chest to protect it from the steady flow of water dripping from my chin.

My chest tightens so I reach for my inhaler and shake it.

*Swoosh!*

Again.

*Swoosh!*

There's a rumble in my stomach. I feel the eruption working its way to my mouth. I scream at Xavier, even though I know he's gone.

"I hate your guts! I hate you! Do you hear me?"

I'm burning with pain and anger. It's Xavier's fault. He needs to know how this feels. I just want to go in his room and set everything on fire.

Wait.

My conversation with Billy rewinds and replays in my head: *Don't let X push you around. . . . If X goes crazy again, hit him where it hurts the most. . . . I mean basketball. He loves hoops more than anything. . . . Remember what I told you about pulling the fire alarm at my dad's job? It totally worked.*

I pull the cell phone from my pocket and hit redial.

"Hello?"

"Billy, it's Lamar."

"Dude, did you get your ball? I told you my way is the fast track."

I clamp my teeth so I won't cry. "I don't want to talk about that."

Silence stalls the conversation.

"Where are you, Washington? What happened? Talk to me."

"It doesn't matter. I'm going to pull the fire alarm at the game tomorrow."

"Are you serious?"

"Yes."

"Wow. Okay, you called the right person. Let's talk tomorrow at Striker's. Ten o'clock."

"I'll be there."

"Don't back out," says Billy.

I wipe blood from my lip. "Trust me, I won't."

## Chapter Seventeen

**M**y mouth hurts and my left eye stings. I
can't sleep. I turn on the radio and plug in
my earphones, then switch the station to heavy
metal. Angry music is what I want to hear.

I listen for hours. I don't remember falling
asleep, but I must've, because I freak when a lead
guitar hits a high note and the singer matches it.
I yank my plugs out and open my eyes. Morning's
here.

In the bathroom, I check out the damage to my
face. My left eye is barely open. It's puffy at the top
and bottom. My lip doesn't look any different from
the outside, but inside it feels bumpy and swollen.

My chest hurts, but it feels a lot better than it did last night.

I breathe in through my nose and exhale from my mouth. This is stupid. I'm not doing these chump exercises today. I get dressed, lace my Jordans, and turn off the light.

Dad's walking around in the living room. I wait for him to retreat to his room, because I'm not doing my chores today either. A pair of sunglasses hides my puffy eye and guards it from the heat of the sun. Our Xavier-loving neighbors shout "Go Coffin!" as I walk by, but I don't return the greeting.

I can't wait to get to Striker's. I'll roll as many strikes as I can, because a strike makes an X light up on the scoreboard and I'll imagine that I'm really lighting up X.

My shades stay on while I get my rental shoes and a lane assignment. I'm on lane fifteen, waiting on Billy. He's late. I check my phone. It's charged and working. I'm thinking about rolling a game to calm my nerves when I hear my name.

Makeda and an older, thin woman with skinny wrists stand near me. The woman smiles, and it takes every muscle in my face to return it. I push my glasses up the bridge of my nose like Dr. Avery does and hope no one says anything about me wearing them.

"Hey, Lamar. What's up with the sunglasses?"

Dang.

"I'm having some problems with my left eye. Lots of light hurts, so I'm wearing these."

"Can I take a look?"

"No! I mean, it'll hurt."

"I'm sorry." She turns to the lady with her. "Lamar, this is Ms. Worthy. Ms. Worthy, Lamar."

"It's nice to meet you, Lamar. Makeda tells me you're a good bowler."

I shrug, and even that hurts. "I'm pretty good."

Ms. Worthy sits next to me and scans the bowling alley. "I used to bowl. It was so much fun. I can't for the life of me remember why I stopped. Maybe I'll start back up again."

I nod. "You should, Ms. Worthy. Lots of old people bowl."

I look at my girl. She's shaking her head, so I flip the switch and work my charm.

"And lots of young people, too, like you and me and Makeda."

The happy returns to my girl's face. She touches me on the shoulder and I wince.

"Are you sure you're okay?"

"Uh-huh."

"Ms. Worthy and I are going to the mall and then to see a movie. Wanna come?"

Double no.

"No thanks. I'm going to hang out here for a while, but have fun."

I walk them to the exit.

"It was nice meeting you, Lamar," says Ms. Worthy.

"You, too. Makeda's like the best person in the world for that counselor position. You'd totally mess up if you didn't hire her."

She smiles, and I open the door for her and my girl. They walk out and I feel like I've done my job.

At eleven o'clock Billy makes his way to lane fifteen. He stops in front of me.

"What's with the shades?"

I take them off and he doesn't budge.

"That's a beauty. Put any ice on it?"

I put them back on. "Can we talk about what we planned to talk about?"

He drops his gear. "Sure. Let's rock and talk, Washington."

Billy sits next to me. "Okay. First of all, are we really going to do this?"

"Yes."

He leans in. "Here's my rule: If you get caught tonight, you don't mention anything about me, got it? I mean ever."

"Yeah."

"Same thing goes for me. If I get caught, I'll never mention your name, understand? My word is good, Washington. Is your word good?"

"Good as yours."

"Cool. Okay, let's talk about specifics. The game starts at five. Plan to meet at the concession stand during halftime."

Billy checks the lanes on both sides of us. "Let's bowl so we don't look suspicious."

I can't focus. I've done nothing to prepare myself to bowl. I hear Billy's ball hit the wood and roll down the lane, but I don't care.

Billy sits next to me. "You remember where the alarm is, don't you?"

I look to the side of me. Billy wipes his hands with his bowling towel. He tilts his head and nods toward the lane.

"Go bowl, Washington. You're too tight. You gotta get some of that off you."

With everything I have, I chuck that twelve-pound ball down the lane. My shoulder and arm throb, but I need that ball to connect with something, just like X's fist did. I've never been so happy to totally annihilate seven pins. The best thing is I get to roll again. I miss everything.

"Tough break, Washington."

"I don't care. Let's finish talking about tonight."

"Sure. Okay, you're going to need a lookout man. That's me. I'm going to stand in the hall near the men's room and make sure nobody comes back there. If I see someone heading that way, I'll give you a signal like a whistle or something, okay?"

"Okay."

"Good. Now, let's get our timing down. As soon as the halftime buzzer sounds and people start crowding the concession stand, we'll make our first move. Go to the bathroom across from the computer room, walk into a stall, and stay there. I'll do the same. We'll stay there until the buzzer sounds for the third quarter to begin."

So far this sounds good. "Okay, then what?"

"Once we know the restroom is clear, I'll leave first to make sure no one is watching. Wait one minute, and then you come out. This way, it won't look like we're together."

I nod. "That makes sense."

"Okay, here comes the important part, Washington. I'm going to have a book with me. I'll slide down the wall not far from the bathroom and pretend to read. Most security people won't bother kids reading. When you come out of the bathroom, if I nod yes, go down the hall and stand by the alarm. If I shake my head, it means we'll have to do it some other time."

"Okay."

Billy gets his ball off the ball return. "So I'll nod and you race to your spot. Once you get there, count to fifty and pull the alarm."

"Okay, then what?"

"Then nothing. You're done. Stay with the crowd and blend in."

"I can do that."

"You better. You'll only get one shot."

Billy paces in front of me. "You're doing the right thing, Washington. He crossed the line and you need to let him know."

I put my hand up toward his face. "I don't need a pep talk. I need a partner."

"I'm your man, bro."

He steps up to the approach line, rolls a spinner down the lane, and kills eight pins. He spares with the second ball.

I stand to leave. "Anything else you need to tell me?"

"Yeah. This is your last chance to back out."

I kick off my bowling shoes. "It's yours, too."

"I'm in," Billy says.

"Then I'll see you tonight."


After bowling I'm not ready to go home, so I drop a few coins in the Indy 500 racing game and take a seat behind the wheel. I hit the gas and shift gears like I'm really in the race. The more I think about what Xavier did, the faster I go. It's not long before I crash into several other cars and my game's over.

I shove more coins in and try again. This time I lose control and smash my car into the wall. I hit the steering wheel with my hand and get up.

Next I try pinball. I flip that ball out, and the machine lights up as the ball makes contact with bumpers.

*Bing. Bing-bing.*

Here comes that ball, straight down the middle, in between my flippers. I nudge the machine to change the ball's path and everything stops. The word TILT lights up. What a rip-off. I try every game in the arcade, but today's just not my day. It's time to go.

## Chapter Eighteen

When I get home, Dad and X are gone. There's a Post-it note stuck on the table with my name on it.

*Lamar,*

*Your brother told me everything. Thanks for volunteering to give me your spot on the mantel, but if you ever want it back, let me know. Here's $5 for admission to the game. See you there.*

*Dad*

I slam Dad's note back on the table. In the kitchen, I pop the top on the chocolate milk and chug until it runs down the sides of my mouth. X drinks this stuff before and after every game. He likes it ice-cold. I thump the top back on the milk and leave it on the counter.

On my way out, I glare at the mantel. X started this war. I'm going to finish it.

Down the street, signs reading BE BACK AFTER THE GAME hang in store windows. A huge banner above the stoplight reads COFFIN YMCA HOOPS IS NUMBER 1!

Now I know why X thinks he's better than me. This town is to blame. The sports fanatics of Coffin have turned him into that pompous, big-headed maggot.

I've still got four blocks to go and I can hear people chanting for Scottsburg. Two blocks from the Y, police direct the steady flow of heavy traffic. People double-park along the street. A big orange sign at the parking lot entrance reads FULL.

Fans march through the YMCA doors like ants. Signs stick in the grass. I hear a band playing. I pay my five bucks and shuffle in. Dad looks intense behind the coach. Mr. Jenks sits next to him. They're both frozen, watching their boys take practice shots.

I get a seat high on the Coffin-side bleachers. I comb the area for Billy. Cheerleaders shout spirit chants from both sides of the gym. They dance to music played by the band until the announcer has us all rise for the "Star-Spangled Banner."

Moments later, the buzzer sounds. The starting five for both Scottsburg and Coffin shake hands and form a circle around midcourt. Loud claps, thunderous stomps, and earsplitting whistles rock the gym. When X takes the floor, I zone in on him like a paid assassin.

He walks with confidence across the court in the brand-new athletic shoes Dad bought him. Why does he always point at Dad and Dad point back before the games starts? Those must be the pro and college scouts sitting in their own cluster between the team benches, nodding at X and writing on their clipboards.

This is what he lives for: the spotlight, the attention. X is in his element, his world.

He can't wait for the first quarter to begin. I can't wait until halftime.

Scooter enters the midcourt circle for a jump ball. When the referee throws the ball into the air, he outjumps the center for Scottsburg, tipping it to Xavier, and the game begins.

Xavier holds up his fist. That's the signal for a play designed to get the ball to Scooter. Coffin's players move to different places on the court. The Scottsburg players form a zone defense, except for one poor guy who has to constantly guard my brother.

Scottsburg's team keeps their hands in the air. They keep their feet planted and move only when the ball moves. Xavier dumps a pass inside to Scooter. He doesn't have a clear shot, so he kicks it back out to X. They set up the play again.

I look for Billy in the crowd. It's impossible to find him. People cram together, shoulder to shoulder on the bleachers. But I know Billy's here. I sense it.

Into the second quarter, I still haven't spotted him. In two minutes, the halftime buzzer will sound. A chill runs through me and I blame it on the air-conditioning. My heartbeat taps Morse code rhythms, but it has to be from the intenseness of the game. I will *not* back out.

A Scottsburg player throws up a prayer from midcourt that misses as the halftime buzzer sounds. Coffin's up by four. An exodus to the concession stand begins. I stand and almost fall over. My legs are weak and wobbly, but I manage to walk down the bleachers.

This is it. I make my way to the gym floor with the moving masses.

"Lamar!"

I unravel at the sound of my name. Dad waves. Now he's signaling me to come to him. Oh no. I rush over, and he hands me a couple bucks.

"Did you get my note?" He stares at my face. "What happened to your eye?"

"It's a long story."

"Did your brother see that?"

"Yes, sir, he saw it."

Dad looks at Mr. Jenks, who's shaking his head, staring at my face.

"I'm sure your brother is going to handle it in a way that I can't. He may pick on you, but he's not going to let anyone else do it. Please bring me a Coke from the concession stand. You can keep the change. Jenks, you want anything?"

Mr. Jenks hands me a fistful of pennies and nickels. "Whatever this will get me."

I check the game clock. Five minutes until halftime is over. I hope Billy doesn't freak out and burn off.

Standing in the concession line takes three long minutes before I reach the counter. I hear basketballs bouncing inside the gym. Cheerleaders chant and clap with sharp precision. The third quarter is about to start and I'm nowhere near where I should be.

"May I help you?"

"Two Cokes, please."

I keep Mr. Jenks's change because I'm not pulling pennies out of my pocket. I pay with Dad's money, grab the drinks, and speed-walk toward the gym.

Coke runs down my wrists. I don't care. I'm late. I hand them the half-empty cups.

"Thanks, Lamar. I've got a feeling it's going to get loud in here during the second half," says Dad.

"Me, too," I say.

I dart through the concession crowd and out of nowhere Billy shows up, walking beside me in stride. We turn the corner and I check over my shoulder to be sure no one follows. Billy talks fast.

"Change of plan. We're late, so three minutes after the third quarter starts, pull the alarm and haul ass. Listen for the referee's whistle. I'll be in this hall, looking out."

My breaths are short, hands are sweaty. "Yeah, okay, looking out."

I take a puff from my inhaler. Billy grabs a tight handful of my shirt.

"Are you going to do this, Washington? 'Cause if you're not . . .'"

"Shut up, Billy. I'm doing it."

"That's better. For a minute there, I thought you were backing out on me."

I puff out my chest. "No way. Not this time. I'm doing this."

He puts his hand on my shoulder and nods. "I'll be right here, bro."

I rush around the corner and stop in front of the fire alarm.

Painted near the top of the red vertical rectangle, in big white letters, the word FIRE reminds me of how hot I am with X. How he tortures me for things that are not my fault. Mom put the note on the mantel, not me. He's the one that's dumb as a bag of rocks, not me. And Dad doesn't have a clue of what goes on at home when he's not there.

He doesn't protect me. Nobody does.

The word ALARM is on the bottom, and that is what I plan to do to my brother. I'm not taking any more beat-downs. I want panic to race through Xavier as I take something important from him. I want him to be devastated, watching people leave his precious basketball game. Yeah, he'll crumple, just like he crumpled Mom's note.

I'm steady on the Pull Down lever. It's ready and waiting. So am I. Sweat seeps from my pores. Inhale. Exhale. Inhale. Exhale. My conscience tries one last time to break me.

Am I making a mistake? I close my eyes. If only I had a sign that I won't regret this. When my eyes open, the letters on the word ALARM are scrambled.

They now spell LAMAR. Whoa.

The third quarter buzzer sounds. I check my watch: five forty-five. I hear cheerleaders and fans, chants and shouts, trumpets and drums. The referee's whistle signals the band to stop playing for the jump ball. Silence.

Something happens. I hear bits and pieces of shouts echoing through the quiet halls.

"Loose ball! Get the ball, Xavier!"

Yeah. That's perfect. Let X get the ball. He can carry it out of the gym in just a few seconds. I place my left fingers on the alarm lever: five forty-seven.

My eyes dart from the fire alarm to my watch.

Thirty seconds.

I didn't want it to come down to this, but you pushed me, Xavier.

Twenty.

You gave me the worst beat-down of my life.

Ten.

And you ripped Mom away from me.

Five forty-eight.

It's your turn to get something taken away.

Eat this, X.

I yank the lever down and watch red lights dance across the walls and floor. A siren blasts so loud, I cover my ears and sprint down the hall. Water spits from the ceiling. First it's slow, then a gush sprays from different directions. Billy didn't mention a sprinkler system. Maybe he didn't know. I keep running and turn the corner.

Where's Billy? It's hard to see through this

hazy waterfall. I can't call for him, but I don't want to leave him either. After all, he's helping me, but where did he go? I dart into the restroom and push each stall door.

"Billy? Billy?"

I dash out and down the hall. Water splashes and soaks my Jordans. Just before I turn the corner to the concession stand, a tall, thin man with YMCA SECURITY stitched on his yellow shirt appears. I slide to a stop.

"Where are you coming from, young man?"

Oh no! Don't panic. Look innocent.

"Nowhere, the bathroom, I was just . . . uh . . ."

I freak and fly, doing my best to outrun him through the wet halls.

"Hey, come back here!"

I switch to overdrive. I can't let him catch me. I can't.

The crowd moves like snails in molasses. Water sprays harder from the ceiling, dousing everything and everybody. People scream as the unexpected cold shower drenches them. They push, argue, and call for loved ones.

I turn sideways to cut through one cluster of Scottsburg fans. I duck low and move with a group of kids. If I can get to the front of this crowd, maybe I'll find Billy.

I'm wheezing. No. *NO!* Not now. My fingers

fumble around in my pocket. Where's my inhaler?
I keep moving, patting my pants.

It must have fallen out of my pocket. I drop
to the ground and crawl. My wheezing becomes
musical, as if I'm sucking in on a harmonica. I yell
and push at people.

"Watch your step! Don't crush my inhaler!"

Someone grabs my arm. I'm about to go off
when I see it's the security guard who was chas-
ing me. My chest tightens and I struggle for air.

"Are you okay?" he asks.

"I'm wheezing. I dropped my inhaler."

A younger security guard jogs over to us. His
shoes squish with every step. He turns to the
guard holding my arm and gives a report.

"Mason, I checked the restrooms and the fire
alarm corridor. All clear."

He opens his hand. "But I did find this thing
floating in the hallway."

Mason cuts his eyes to me. "Take a look at what
Greg found."

## Chapter Nineteen

The crowd closes in. It's harder to breathe. They mumble and speculate about what's going on. My name is mentioned over and over. Mason takes my inhaler out of Greg's hand and dangles it in my face.

"Is this yours? If it is, you better take it. You don't look so good, kid."

I take my inhaler and shove the mouthpiece between my lips. I close my eyes as the mist works its way down my throat. Come on. Work, medicine.

Mason turns to the crowd. "Move back, people. He needs air. Give him room." He whispers to me, "I'll call an ambulance."

I open my eyes and shake my head. "Just let me sit for a minute. Then I can go home."

Mason whispers again. "Are you able to walk?"

"Yeah, I think so."

He moves my arm toward the Y. "Good. Come with me, son."

Greg and Mason sandwich me between them, Mason holding my left arm, Greg holding my right. I scan the crowd for Dad. I've got to get out of this before he sees me. I turn to Mason.

"Can I just talk to you a minute?"

"We'll talk about it when the police get here."

I slow down. "Police?"

Sirens interrupt my thoughts. We both turn as two fire trucks roll into the parking lot. Firemen rush by us into the Y. I jerk away from Mason and Greg, not running but frozen in fear.

"I didn't do anything," I say.

Mason takes a step closer and points his finger an inch from my nose.

"I hope you're not thinking of doing something stupid, because if I have to chase you again, I will drag you back here by something that will hurt a lot more than an arm. Get moving."

Voices call out from the enormous crowd.

"Lamar, what's going on?"

"Hey, Lamar, are you in trouble?"

Mason looks over at his partner. "Greg, take

care of this crowd. Tell them the game is canceled."

Greg lets go of my arm. "I'm on it."

I wish the ground would crack open and swallow me, especially right now since Makeda and her friend Ms. Worthy are up ahead. What are they doing here? Oh, snap! I forgot. Makeda comes to all of the games.

They wipe water from their faces and watch me take my walk of shame back into the YMCA. Just before I pass them, I hear Ms. Worthy asking questions.

"Makeda, isn't that your friend? Lamar, right?"

A slide show of emotions plays across Makeda's face before she turns to Ms. Worthy.

"Lamar's not really my friend. We go to the same school. He gets a kick out of playing bad pranks on me. I guess he got me again." Tears roll down her cheeks.

I reach for her hand. "No, Makeda, you've got it all wrong."

Mason puts a hand on my shoulder. "You can explain to her later. Keep moving."

I try to look back at her but can't. Mason pushes the YMCA door open, and the noise inside scares me. Although the sprinkler system and alarm are off, there's a whole new chaos going on. Firemen slosh through water, open doors, and call to anyone still inside. The fire chief guards the front entrance and holds his two-way radio as his crew updates him through their walkie-talkies.

"All clear in north corridor—over!"

"All clear in the gymnasium—over!"

Mason and I stay out of their way and walk to his office. His door is wide open, and I can tell he's not happy. He kicks a chair away from the wall.

"Park it."

I do, and look around. Behind a big desk are four small televisions mounted high in the middle of the wall. Mason checks them before walking to his window and opening it.

"Aren't you Xavier Washington's little brother? Lamar, right?"

"Yes, sir."

"You pulled that fire alarm, didn't you?"

I don't answer. I'm too scared to answer. Mason walks to the window and looks over his shoulder at me as he points to four televisions perched on the wall.

"That's high-tech surveillance equipment. Cameras don't lie. You're going to stick with the silent treatment?"

How stupid! Why didn't we think of cameras? Where's Billy? It's just a matter of time before this guy watches that tape. Dang. There's nothing I can do.

"I pulled it."

The office door opens. Two firemen and two police officers walk in. I'm trembling as they eyeball me. I can't take the embarrassment, so I lower my head and stare at the carpet. A set of wet, black rubber boots moves into my view.

"Look at me, son. What's your name?"

I slowly raise my head and look into the face of a very angry fireman. "Lamar Washington."

He takes off his hat and wipes the sweat from his brow.

"Do you realize people could have been hurt, Lamar? Ever heard of a panic stampede? Someone could have been killed. Pulling a fire alarm is never going to be considered funny, cute, or a prank by the Fire Department. It's a crime and you're in trouble, son."

I feel sick. "I'm sorry. I didn't mean to . . ."

"I don't want to hear 'I'm sorry.' When the Fire Department gets a call, we treat each response as if lives are at stake. After what you did today, I don't think you take our job seriously, Lamar."

"That's not true. I really do," I say.

The fireman gets in my face. "Don't ever let me hear the words *Lamar Washington* and *fire alarm* in the same sentence again."

I don't blink. "Yes, sir."

He puts his hat on and tips it at Mason. "We've turned off the electricity." He looks at the televisions on the wall and points to them. "You must have a backup generator or something?"

Mason nods. "Only for my surveillance equipment."

"Good. With all of this water and the humidity in the building, I'd say you've got less than an hour before the heat will be unbearable. Leave the electricity off for a few days, but get this water out before mildew and mold set in. Good job, Mason."

Both firemen shake hands with the police officers and Mason before they leave. Mason frowns at me and grabs the walkie-talkie clipped to his hip.

"Greg, please find Xavier Washington's dad and bring him in—over."

A voice answers back. "Already found him. He's on his way."

"Thanks, Greg. Over and out."

My neck hurts from holding my head down, but I'm not looking up. I can't believe he said *Xavier's dad*. Isn't he my dad, too? I sit for what feels like three days before fear resurfaces in the form of a fist pounding on the door.

*Bam, bam, bam!*

I know Dad's anger when I hear it. One of the officers opens the door. It's Dad and Xavier. Dad seems surprised to see the police and even more surprised to see me sitting in the middle of everything. He turns to the officer who opened the door.

"What's going on here?"

"That's what we're trying to find out. Are you the suspect's father?"

Dad's eyes switch to high beam. "Suspect? Yes, he's my son. What did he do?"

Xavier locks in on me. His expression is murder. I can't imagine what my expression looks like.

"I'm Officer Perkins." He points at the other office. "That's my partner, Officer Dyson. We'd like to ask your son a few questions."

Dad nods. Officer Perkins gets started.

"What's your name, son?"

"Lamar."

"Lamar, you want to tell me what happened?"

I would've, but Dad doesn't let me answer.

"I can tell you exactly what happened. He should have been in the gym watching his brother shoot lights out, but instead, he was, he was . . . I don't know *what* he was doing!"

Dad's out of control. I've never seen him this angry. Will he be this tough on Xavier when he finds out he blacked my eye? I doubt it. Dad keeps yelling. The more he yells, the angrier I get. I'm a volcano, and if he doesn't stop yelling at me, I'm going to blow. And then Dad says the one thing that starts the eruption.

"I just can't believe you pulled that alarm, Lamar! I mean, not after all of the things your brother does for you. We were just talking about how Xavier's going to handle that business with your black eye. That's what brothers do. They take up for one another."

If Dad doesn't stop talking, I swear, I'm going to explode. My eyes stay glued to his face as he paces in front of the door. Finally he walks up on me and points a finger in my face.

"Let's just skip all of the preliminary stuff. Lamar, did you pull that alarm?"

"Yes! I pulled the stupid alarm and I'd do it again! Because I want X to know I hate his guts, okay? There. I said it."

Xavier frowns and points a stiff finger at me. "*You* pulled the alarm? You knew how important this was for me, Lamar! You ruined everything!"

I holler back. "You ruined everything first, Xavier! Dad, why don't you ask him how I got this black eye? He should know, since he gave it to me! Is that what brothers do? Is it?"

Heads turn to face X. As Dad's eyes move to the corner where Xavier stands, his face grimaces even more.

"You put your hands on your brother?"

Officer Perkins clears his throat. "Let's take a breath, okay? Mr. Washington, I'll let you handle that situation at home. Lamar, you're going to watch the surveillance tape and walk me through exactly what you did."

"Yes, sir."

Mason moves to a high-tech area in his office. Four small televisions with video recorders beneath them are still filming the hallways of the YMCA. He pushes buttons on a remote and the pictures change. Now all the TVs show the time as 5:40 and today's date stamped at the top of the screen.

Everyone stands in front of the surveillance televisions. Officers Perkins and Dyson squeeze between Xavier, Dad, and me as Mason puts the remote on his desk and explains how everything works.

"Okay, Lamar, we're going to watch the computer room hall first, because you had to pass it on your way to the fire alarm. And it will give us a timeline."

We stare at an empty hall on the monitor for several minutes. Suddenly, Billy and I show up. Officer Perkins goes berserk.

"Stop the tape!"

He folds his arms and gets in my face. "Please tell me that is *not* Billy Jenks."

I don't answer.

## Chapter Twenty

Officer Perkins mumbles and paces. "You didn't mention anything about an accomplice. What are you doing hanging out with Billy Jenks? Don't you know he's trouble?"

I don't know what to say.

"Answer him!" Dad yells.

I squint at Officer Perkins. "You're wrong about Billy. He was just my lookout guy. He promised to give me a signal if someone came down the hall. That's it."

Officer Perkins shakes his head. "I know Billy very well, Lamar. There's no such thing as 'that's it' when he's involved."

I panic. "Well, it is *this* time. I swear. He was only there to make sure my dad didn't come around the corner and catch me pulling the alarm."

Xavier steps toward me. "You're lying, Lamar! You are *so* dead!"

Officer Perkins points at my brother. "Xavier, sit down! Let me handle this, please."

Dad takes Xavier by the arm and drags him to a row of chairs against the wall.

Mason refocuses us. "Okay, Lamar, you said Billy was your lookout guy?"

I nod. "That's exactly what I'm telling you. I didn't know the alarm was connected to a sprinkler system. I bet Billy didn't either. He probably freaked just like I did and ran outside. I was on my way to find him when you caught me."

Officer Perkins shakes his head. "Mason, turn the tape back on. Lamar, talk me through what I'm watching."

I nod again. "Sure."

As the picture comes in, it shows me and Billy in the hall, and I tell everything about that afternoon.

"We stopped to go over last-minute details. I got nervous and Billy thought I was backing out. I promised him I wasn't, and he promised to be in the hall for me, looking out."

I cut my eyes to Dad and X. Dad is statue still.

Xavier bites his bottom lip. I stand closer to Officer Perkins, just in case Xavier comes at me.

Mason nods. "Okay, I'm going to switch screens. The second television records activities around the fire alarm."

He reaches for his remote, but Officer Perkins grabs his wrist. "Wait."

All eyes turn back to the television screen and watch Billy pull a nail file from his back pocket. He checks the hall one more time before walking up to the computer room door. He inserts the nail file in the lock, jiggles it back and forth, then leans in to listen. I can tell he hears something, because he stops and turns the knob. The door opens. Billy goes in and shuts the door behind him.

I'm paralyzed, physically and mentally. I can't figure out what's going on. This wasn't part of the plan.

Officer Perkins slams his hand on top of Mason's desk.

"Stop the tape!"

He turns to me. "Why is Billy picking the lock on the computer room door, Lamar?"

My breaths shorten as reality unfolds in front of me. Billy had *another* plan, totally separate from mine. *Which he conveniently forgot to mention.*

Officer Perkins puts his hand on my chair. "Lamar, I asked you a question."

I shake my head, shrug, show Officer Perkins the palms of my hands, and tell the truth.

"I don't know. We didn't talk about this. He never said anything about going into the computer room. He's supposed to be in the hall looking out like he promised."

Officer Perkins sighs. "I've got a bad feeling about this, Lamar." He turns to Mason. "Switch to the computer room camera."

Mason presses buttons on his remote. The video shows a windowless room with desks and laptop computers. Billy enters. He scans, lifts his shirt, and removes a square object wrapped in plastic.

"What the heck is that?" I ask.

Mason gets closer to the television. His eyes widen. "You gotta be kidding me!"

He dashes out of the room. I call to him.

"What? What's going on?"

When Mason doesn't answer, I stare at the screen and watch Billy pull the plastic off a new black gym bag. He unzips it and quickly fills the bag with laptops. The fire alarm goes off and water pours from the ceiling. Billy zips the bag, reaches into his back pocket, and pulls out a baseball cap to cover his head. He stands and walks to the door.

My eyes bulge. I point at the screen. "He's stealing the computers!"

The camera continues to scan the room but pauses at the computer room door. My body tightens as I look through the tinted glass and watch the replay of my terrible first encounter with Mason. I watch Billy cup his hands to the glass and witness my drama. Once I run and Mason chases me, Billy opens the computer room door and leaves.

My heart pumps double time. I whip my head to the side to see the expression on my father's face. He won't look at me. I turn back to Officer Perkins.

"Billy said he was going to be my lookout guy. He promised. He helped me plan my every move. I thought he was my friend."

Officer Perkins turns on his radio but raises an eyebrow at me. "Do you *still* think he's your friend?" He pulls the radio to his mouth. "This is Perkins, badge five-four-three-nine. I need an officer to bring in Billy Jenks for questioning on a possible robbery. We'll also need a search warrant for his place of residence to hopefully recover four stolen computers, over." He turns back to me.

"I'm one-hundred-percent sure you had nothing to do with the robbery, but pulling a fire alarm without cause is a crime." He pulls a pair of handcuffs from his belt and reaches for my right wrist.

"Lamar Washington, I'm placing you under arrest."

*Clink. Clink.*

My body tightens. "Dad, help me! It was just a stupid prank!"

Dad's eyes water. His hands rest on his hips. He shoves them into his pocket. Seconds later, his arms fold across his chest. And then, they rest on his hips again.

"There's nothing I can do, Lamar. Pulling a fire alarm is not a prank. It's a crime."

"But I didn't know!"

Officer Perkins asks for silence as he reads me my rights. "Do you understand what I just read, Lamar?"

I wipe my eyes. "Yes, sir."

He turns to Dad. "I'm sorry, Mr. Washington. I have to book him. You can meet us downtown. He should be ready in an hour or so."

Perkins and Dyson escort me down the flooded hall. We approach the exit doors. I look out at the crowd of soggy people standing in the grass, waiting in the parking lot. Officer Perkins opens the door. A thousand sets of eyes stare at me.

Coming out in handcuffs makes me instant gossip, tried and found guilty by appearance.

My face warms in shame. I hear two women whisper as I pass by.

"His mother would turn over in her grave."

I tighten my jaw so I don't cry. Sergio steps out of the crowd and stands in front of me.

"Lamar, what happened?"

He's dressed in a Holiday World T-shirt and cap.

I shake my head. "I'm sorry, bro. I can't go. I'll make it up to you."

"You can't make it up to me! It's my birthday, Lamar. You messed up my birthday!"

Officer Perkins points at Sergio. "Move."

I can't hold it any longer. I burst into tears in front of the whole town of Coffin.

Officer Perkins palms my afro and pushes it down as I bend to sit in the backseat. "Watch your head, son."

The siren blares. Reflections of revolving red and blue lights flash off cars and clothing as we leave the parking lot. The silence inside the squad car is louder than the music at Striker's.

At the police station, I'm fingerprinted and photographed before they allow me to leave with Dad. Officer Perkins tells us that the judge has referred me to a resolution council called the Coffin Accountability Board. I see them tomorrow, and they will hand down my punishment.

As Officer Perkins and Dad talk, I wonder if this Accountability Board is going to send me away. In the middle of my freak-out, Dad grabs a handful of my shirt.

"Let's go."

Xavier's in the front seat. I slide into the back. Once we're inside, Xavier begins to talk, but Dad holds up his hand and breaks X off in one low tone.

"I don't want to hear from you right now."

No radio, no conversation, nothing. X fixes the mirror on his sun visor to stare at me. I try to avoid his looks, but it's so hard. I'm in trouble. I'm in big trouble.

Dad pulls up to the curb. I rush up the steps. Xavier sprints after me. Before I can open the door, he snatches my collar and rams me against the outside wall. I struggle to break free. There's evil in his eyes, and I brace for another painful beat-down.

Dad's huge arm appears on Xavier's shoulder. He spins him around and pins him to the screen door. "It's over. Do you hear me? All of this pay-back mess is over."

Dad gets in Xavier's face. "If you *ever* put your hands on your brother again, I'm going to put my hands on you. Are you taking your medication? Answer me, Xavier!"

Tears flow down my brother's face. "It makes me sleepy. And it makes me sick to my stomach. I can't play ball like that." His head lowers. "It doesn't matter, Dad. The scouts were there today. They won't come back. I'll never pass algebra. Lamar ruined everything."

Dad fumbles with his keys to unlock the front door. "Stop saying that! Everything is *not* ruined! We'll figure out something, but right now, bring me your medicine!"

X shuffles to his room. Dad turns to me. I tremble, watching his chest move up and down as air enters and exits his flared nostrils. He lifts his finger toward my bedroom door.

"Go wait for me."

I sit on the edge of my unmade bed and wait. I'm wheezing like crazy, so I take a quick puff of my inhaler. I've got yesterday's clothes sprawled on the floor. My feet are still wet inside my shoes. I want to take them off, but I'm scared to do anything.

Dad appears in my doorway with Xavier's prescription bottle in his hand. He scans my room, comes inside, and sits at my desk. With arms folded across his chest, he fires the first question.

"Do you have any idea what you've done?"

"It wasn't supposed to go down like that, Dad. I didn't know about the sprinklers."

"Your brother is devastated, and rightfully so. Your boneheaded, idiotic prank wasn't funny. Worst of all, you've labeled yourself. Do you know what that means?"

I look at him. "What?"

"People will whisper about you for the rest of your life. They'll call you a thug, a juvenile delinquent, a troublemaker, bad news."

I stand and pace. "That's not fair. I'm not a thug. A guy can only get dogged so much before he can't take anymore. I had enough, Dad, and I wanted X to get the message."

I plop on my bed again, grab a handful of my blanket, and twist it.

"I had to get even with him for what he did to me."

Dad's eyebrows move closer together. "You're talking about your eye, right?"

I feel the tears coming from behind my eyes. The wells fill before I have a chance to prepare.

"Did you really think I'd volunteer my space on the mantel? Did you? I'm not going to tell you what X did. Let me show you."

I yank off my shirt and watch Dad's expression change from curiousity to shock. He glares at my bruised chest and sides. Before he can say anything, I put my shirt back on because those scars don't hurt nearly as bad as what I'm about to show him.

I gently lift Mom's Post-it from my nightstand and give it to him. His face wrinkles worse than the crumpled edges of the tiny note. His eyes tear up, but I'm too angry to care.

"How do you think that happened, Dad?"

I can't hold it. I clamp my teeth to hold on, but I can't. The longer I stare at Mom's note, the harder I cry. The uncontrolled outburst angers me. I wipe my face hard with the bottom of my shirt.

"Why can't you see what's up? X has everything. That note was all I had of Mom, but X took that, too. And what happens? I get blamed. I'm a thug now because I fought back."

"Why didn't you talk to me, Lamar?"

"About what? About who? Your beloved Xavier the Basketball Savior? I try to make you proud, Dad, but all you care about is my breathing treatments and my inhaler."

"That's not true, Lamar. I talk to you about a lot of things."

"No you don't! What have we ever done together? When have we just kicked it, you know, sat around and talked like you and X do all the time?"

"I talk to you about bowling together, I ask about Sergio, and—"

I cut him off. I've got so much to say and I need to say it.

"I made the honor roll every semester last year. I showed you my report card. Where was my celebration steak dinner? Mom would have done something. She believed in me."

I take her note from his hand. "She even put it in writing."

Dad grimaces. "So she would have approved of how you handled this situation? You think your mom would be proud of you right now, Lamar?"

I try to reply. "Mom would say . . . I'm sure she would say . . ."

The clock rings midnight in the living room.

*Clang!* . . . *Clang!* . . . *Clang!* . . .

Each chime sounds like my conscience. Would Mom be proud?

*No . . . no . . . no . . .*

I collapse on my bed, grab my head with both hands, and wail it out. Dad's fingers slide across my shoulders, and we cry together.

"I miss her, too, Lamar. I miss her so much."

We sit on my bed, shoulder to shoulder. I tell Dad everything. I tell him about my drama with Sergio. I even mention how Dr. Avery refused to give me any supermeds to play soccer.

"Soccer? Why would you try out for soccer?"

I begin to cry again. "See, there was this girl."

A half grin slides across Dad's face. "Say no more. Girls will make you do stupid stuff like stand on your head and recite the Pledge of Allegiance. Yeah, I did that in fourth grade."

Dad spaces on me. He's got that checked-out glaze in his eyes. I clear my throat and he checks back in.

"Anyway, when did you start liking girls, Lamar? We haven't even talked about girls yet."

"Dad, I'm thirteen. This isn't fourth grade. You're, like, on the late show. Makeda was my woman and I lost her. She'll probably never speak to me again. I totally messed up her life."

We sit on my bed, all talked out. I feel empty but better, but Dad looks out of it.

"Dad, did you hear what I said?"

"Yeah, I heard everything. I'm just upset that you believed I love Xavier more than you. You've gone through some serious grown-up things all by yourself. I'm sorry you didn't feel comfortable talking to me first. But I'll promise you one thing. Xavier will take his medicine every day from now on. I'll make sure of it. Go to bed, Lamar."

He stands to leave.

I sit up. "That's it?"

"Oh no. We'll talk about this more after the meeting with the Coffin Accountability Board. I am putting you on lockdown until further notice. Don't ask me for any special privileges, mall trips, nothing. And give me that bowling pass."

Tears come back. I open my wallet and give it to him. He clicks the light and shuts the door.

## Chapter Twenty-one

*A* clap of thunder awakens me from a dream of bowling lights out at Striker's, one strike after another, in perfect rhythm, with everybody in Coffin rooting for me. I try to drift back into oblivion when a strike of lightning scares the bejeebies out of me. It's raining. Just what this town needs to remind them of my screwup.

I sit on the edge of my bed and notice the *Coffin Chronicle* at the foot of my door. I grab it and glare at the front page. I'm looking down at my handcuffs in the photo, but it's clearly me. Next to my picture, X has taken a marker and written "Superstar." I toss it back on the floor just as someone knocks.

"Yeah."

It's Dad. "Lamar, get up. You're going to be late for your meeting."

"Yes, sir."

Dang. How could I forget about those accountability people? What are they going to do to me? Will they send me away?

I get out of bed, take a quick shower, dress in my church clothes, and groom my fro until it's round and perfect. I spray on a little cologne but not too much. My teeth are pearly white and I practice looking innocent and saying "I'm sorry" in the mirror.

As Dad drives down Eighth Avenue, he schools me on how to act and what to say and what not to say. Just as I settle in for what I'm thinking is going to be a long ride, he pulls into the library parking lot.

"What are we doing here?"

He turns off the ignition and opens his door. "This is where the Accountability Board meets. Get moving so we're not late."

We walk to a room in the back of the library and sign in.

The place is packed with adults. Once we take a seat, everybody in the room does the same. A woman with short white hair calls my name.

"Yes, ma'am?"

She shakes my hand. "I'm Lenora Grimms, the moderator for this meeting and a member of the Coffin Community Accountability Board. These other people are business owners and leaders in our community who also volunteer as board members. Okay, Lamar, it is our understanding that your family has declined the services of an attorney. Whom have you brought with you for this meeting?"

"My dad, Isaac Washington."

"Welcome, Mr. Washington. Let's begin."

Ms. Grimms reads the charges against me and states why the Community Accountability Board is involved. The committee members ask me why I pulled the alarm and how I feel now. I'm totally embarrassed answering them, but I stand and tell them the truth.

"I pulled the alarm because I had too much drama going on and I couldn't handle it. The last straw came when my brother, Xavier, hit me. I had an opportunity to get even with him, so I did."

"And what do you think about the alarm incident now?" asks Ms. Grimms.

"I wish I had done something different, like scrub the toilet with his toothbrush and then put it back in the holder."

Two board members fake coughs. I know

they're trying to hold back big globs of laugh-out-loud. I'm finished, so I take my seat.

Ms. Grimms writes on her tablet and then turns to me.

"Lamar, what do you think would be a *fair* punishment?"

Dad lets out a big sigh and turns his face toward the door. He doesn't believe in allowing kids to pick their consequences. I shrug and try to sound responsible.

"I don't know. I guess I should have to help fix the damages, if there were any."

"There were," says Ms. Grimms.

A board member raises his hand, and Ms. Grimms points to him. "Yes, please stand, Mr. Simpson. You have the floor."

"Hello, Lamar, I'm John Simpson. I own the dry cleaning service on Twelfth Street. I was at the game when you pulled the alarm. I think you should be ordered to help clean up the YMCA. Then you can understand the magnitude of your actions. That's all I have to say."

Ms. Grimms stands. "Anyone else?"

I cut my eyes left to right. All hands stay down.

"Lamar, you and your father may leave the room while the board finalizes their decision. We'll come get you when we're finished."

Dad and I stand outside the meeting room door, in silence, for what feels like a year but is only ten minutes. The door opens and Ms. Grimms invites us back in. We take our seats. My heart pounds in my chest. Ms. Grimms hands me a piece of paper.

"Lamar Washington, we hereby order you to assist in the restoration of Coffin's YMCA and pay a monetary fine in the amount of two hundred dollars. I have phoned the judge and conveyed our recommendation, and he has approved it."

Dad freaks. They're speaking in his native tongue of Wallet, and he's not going to wait for Ms. Grimms to give him the floor. He stands and waves his hands like a madman.

"Excuse me! Did you say two hundred dollars? I don't have that kind of money."

Ms. Grimms stays calm. "It's not your problem, Mr. Washington. It's Lamar's."

Dad takes his seat and puts an arm around my chair.

Ms. Grimms continues. "Lamar, you'll have six months from today to pay your fine, and tomorrow you will report to the YMCA to begin your community service. On behalf of the Coffin Community Accountability Board, let me say that we hope this is the last time we meet under these circumstances. The people in this room care and believe you can make a change for the better. If no one has anything further to add, this meeting is adjourned."

In the car, Dad gives me the silent treatment again. As soon as he pulls up to the house, I go to my room and climb back into the bed. I just want everything and everybody to go away and leave me alone.

The phone rings. Dad tells X not to answer it. It keeps ringing and ringing. He must have unplugged the answering machine. Finally, I hear Dad answer the phone and tell the caller I've been punished and they need to get over it. That's followed by a slam-down of the receiver.

Someone knocks.

"Yeah."

"Lamar, come eat. I need to talk to you and Xavier."

If I walk any slower I'll be moving backward. But I make it to the table. Dad has an angry expression on his face. X looks nervous. Dad bangs the table with his fist and I chump-jump.

"I want this situation fixed. You are brothers, and I expect you to start acting like brothers. Because if you don't, I'm going to continue to strip away the things that are the most important to you until you figure it out. And if that means I have to strip you down until you have nothing left but each other, then so be it."

When he gets through forking out new chores, I want to scream. He hands me my equipment and sends Xavier to the garage to get his.

It's tough being the L-Train with a pink feather duster hanging from your caboose. I'm Molly Maid and Mr. Clean all wrapped into one dusty chump. I've got everybody's chores inside the house until next Tuesday. Bathrooms, bedrooms, every room is now my job.

Xavier's got everything outside. He has to rake, water Mom's garden, and mow the lawn. Plus I overheard Dad's private conversation with Xavier. Dad's voice rang off every wall in X's room. But when his voice cracked, and he told X that what he was about to do hurt him just as much as it was going to hurt X, I knew my brother was in prime-time trouble.

Dad confiscated his basketball and banned him from playing in the YMCA makeup game. X went ballistic but quickly got a clue. Since it's raining, Dad is making him stay in his room and study algebra.

I wrap a bandana around my fro to keep the dust out as I feather-beat Dad's bedroom furniture. With this bottle of Formula 409 clipped to my belt, I could model for *Janitors-R-Us* magazine.

While cleaning Dad's bathroom, I think about

my boy. I bet he had a terrible time at Holiday World. Maybe he didn't go at all. I'm going to sneak a call to him. I owe him a major apology. I've got to make that up to him.

After dinner Dad goes in his room. I hide the phone under my shirt and stroll to my bedroom to call Sergio. I dial the number and wait.

He answers. "Hello?"

"Sergio?"

"What do you want, Lamar?"

"I needed to talk to you about something, bro."

After a short silence, he uses four words to break me.

"I ain't your bro."

*Click.*

I still have the receiver in my hand. I'm listening to the dial tone buzzing in my ear. He dissed me. Sergio left me to talk to Mr. Buzz.

Maybe if I can just explain myself to Makeda, she'll forgive me. I dial her number. My left knee bobs up and down as her phone rings.

"Phillips residence."

"May I speak to Makeda?"

"Who's calling?"

Uh-oh. "Hello, Mrs. Phillips. This is Lamar. I just wanted to apologize to her."

I hear her call Makeda to the telephone. I also hear Makeda's response.

"Tell him I don't want to talk to him anymore."

"Lamar . . ."

"It's okay, Mrs. Phillips. I heard her. Thanks anyway. Good-bye."

Life-sized posters of Bubba, Usher, and Beyoncé cover my walls. They're staring at me as if they know I messed up and probably just lost my girl. Even when I turn away, I can feel them dead-eyeing me.

"What are you looking at!"

Holy crackers and cream cheese, I'm talking to posters. I've got to get out of here.

I shuffle to the kitchen, start the dishwasher, then move to the living room. As I dust above the mantel, I consider knocking all of Xavier's trophies over. A twinge in my stomach freezes me. As I wait for the pain to pass, Xavier's trophies are all in my face. I'm eye level with the inscriptions and dates on the little gold plates on the bases.

I remember when he got this little trophy in fifth grade for making thirty straight free throws. And this one's for the best three-point percentage on his middle school team. These two are from his last year of middle school, when he crushed the school records in points scored and assists.

But this monster trophy is the one he got after his first season on junior varsity. He was the youngest guy to make the state all-star team. And the team named him MVP. As I push to my tiptoes to dust this trophy, the absolute worst thought becomes clear and the feather duster falls from my hand. I remove the bandana from my head.

I didn't just pull a fire alarm. I didn't just pull a stupid prank. I pulled the plug on my brother's dream and completely ruined his life.

Thanks to me, there may not be any more basketball trophies for X. Xavier the Basketball Savior will just be some tall freak with shame in his game because he can't pass algebra. And if he's telling the truth about the scouts not coming back, my brother's stuck in Coffin, working at the local grocery store or something, with no chance of ever getting out.

All because I pulled the fire alarm.

My shoulders slump in disgrace as I get my head around what I've done to him. An apology is weak and won't fix a thing. No wonder he hates me.

Sergio's right. I messed up everything.

## Chapter Twenty-two

*E*arly Thursday morning, I get my chores done and head to the Y. Ms. Ledbetter is out in her garden. She looks up at me, shakes her head, then goes back to gardening.

Ms. Gibson is about to sit in her rocker when I pass. She frowns when she sees me but doesn't speak. I've always wanted them to keep their mouths closed, but not this way.

Five minutes later, I'm standing in front of the YMCA. A car pulls into the parking lot. It's Mason and Greg. Two other guys get out of the back-seat. They all walk toward me with lunch pails in their hands and rubber boots on their feet. I hear my name and the words *fire alarm* before they reach me.

"Good morning, Lamar," says Mason.

"Good morning."

"Hi, Lamar," says Greg.

"Hey."

The other two guys don't speak. Mason unlocks the front doors. Water and heat spill out from inside the building. Mason leaves the doors propped open.

"Lamar, follow me to the back. I'll get you a mop and a bucket so you can get started."

Mason leads me past the computer room and around the corner where I pulled the alarm. My chest tightens as I get closer. He unlocks a door and pulls out a mop, a bucket, and a hall barrier to block water from the other halls. He hands me the mop and bucket.

"You're familiar with this hall, so you can start here. Mop up the water, then squeeze the water out into the bucket. Once the bucket's full, dump the water in the sink in that room where I got the mop. Then start over again. Any questions?"

"No, sir."

Mason puts his hand on my shoulder. "I'll be back to check on you later."

I look him in the eye. "I'm sorry. I just wanted to tell you that."

His eyebrows rise. "I bet you are, kid. And you're lucky, too. That Jenks boy got six months in boot camp for stealing those laptops. I showed the surveillance tape to the judge and Jenks's attorney did a plea bargain."

I can barely breathe. "Six months? Dang."

I've filled my bucket five times with water and emptied it, and I'm still in the same hallway. The more I try to avoid looking at the fire alarm, the more I see it.

I buy a Coke and some cheese crackers out of the machine. I didn't bring a lunch, since I'll only be here until noon, but I'm starving. I've got fifteen minutes until I can go home and start my other job as Holly Housecleaner.

I finally manage to mop the water to the end of the hall. It's noon, and my arms are cooked spaghetti. My Jordans are soaked again. I find Mason and the other guys in the gym.

"Uh, it's noon and I have to go," I say.

Mason nods. "Sure. See you tomorrow."

"Yes, sir."

I walk to the front entrance and hear them snickering. I won't turn around. I won't.

As I pass two men on the sidewalk, they do double takes. I walk faster. Colorful dots of confetti line the streets near the Y. GO COFFIN YMCA! signs lie broken in half on top of trash cans throughout the neighborhood. A ripped good-luck banner dangles from a telephone pole. I walk with my head down. Maybe I didn't steal any laptops, but by the looks of this town, I might have snatched something even more valuable.

I'm at the corner between Makeda's house and Striker's. She wouldn't talk to me last night. Maybe she wants an apology in person. I pick up my pace at the thought of seeing her. I push past the soccer fields but cut my eyes to the hole in the chain-link fence. Soon I'm at the sidewalk that leads to her house.

Her grandma sits on the porch. She waves and I wave back.

"Come on up here," she says, signaling me to join her on the porch.

I'm halfway there when Makeda appears at the screen door. I stop and wait as my heart thumps hard, like too much bass in car speakers. My girl steps outside, and I can't wait to tell her I'm sorry. Just as I restart my walk, Makeda takes her grandma's hand, leads her inside, and shuts the door.

I'm blinking a thousand times a second. I will not cry. Forget about her. She hates me.

I run to Striker's parking lot. It's times like this

when Striker's would help me. I'd roll a few games and get my head on straight.

But I can't go into Striker's.

On top of everything else, I'm wheezing again. I snatch my inhaler from my pocket. My first instinct is to throw it as far as I can. But that won't make my asthma go away. I take a puff and sit on the curb. Someone opens the door and walks out. For a quick moment, I can hear the sounds of people bowling and having fun inside.

Look at me. I slam my brainless brother for his below-sea-level grades. I slam Sergio for kickin' it with a girl who uses him for money. Well, ladies and gentlemen, I take great disappointment in introducing Lamar Washington, hands down, no questions asked, the dumbest sucker ever.

My wheezing stops, so I head home. On my way, I pass two big men. They say something about the Y. I don't respond. They call me names and I walk faster. Finally I put the key in the door and turn the knob.

"Is that you, Lamar?" Dad's on the couch.

"Yes, sir."

I struggle to lift my feet. My arms hurt but not nearly as much as my feelings.

"Dad, can I talk to you a minute?"

"Yeah, sure."

I sit next to him and stare at the floor.

"You were right. Everybody hates me. Everybody."

He doesn't respond. I keep talking.

"I thought if I just apologized, things would be okay. But nobody wants to hear me. The hardest problem I have is dealing with how Billy played me like a punk. And I let him. But why me, Dad? I thought we were going to be . . . friends. Now I'm the butt of Coffin."

"You need to talk to Billy," says Dad. "If you don't, it could happen again."

I turn to him. "No way. Besides, he's in some boot camp. I can't call, and I won't write him either."

"Then go see him, Lamar. Talk to Billy face-to-face, man-to-man."

I shrug. "I'm sure there's more than one boot camp in Indiana."

Dad rubs his neck. "If you want to do this, I'll take you, but I'm not going to do your homework. Find Billy. He has your answers."

# Chapter Twenty-three

Monday, Mason and his two helpers lay the new wood floor for the basketball court. They call me to help. I stay late to help them finish without them asking me. Mason shares his lunch with me, and Greg buys me a Coke.

On Tuesday, the new basketball court is ready for the basketball team to practice for the makeup game against Scottsburg. The team walks in as I'm leaving for the day.

"Well, well, if it isn't Lamar Washington. I thought X beat your brains out," says the equipment manager.

Scooter Jenks bumps me on his way by. "You should have known better than to hang out with my brother. Billy's a butt wipe—and you are, too, for what you did to us."

Any other time I'd fire something back, but Scooter's right.

"I'm sorry for messing up the game, Scooter."

He stops and half grins at me. "Well, that's one thing you and my brother don't have in common. He'd never apologize. Tell X to call me."

I grin back. "Okay."

On my way home, I scan everywhere. I got hit with a rock this morning, but I didn't see where it came from or who threw it. Down the sidewalk a man in a wheelchair rolls toward me. He slows down and gives me a hard look.

"You pulled the alarm at the Y last week, didn't you?"

My head lowers. "Yes, sir."

"My wife and I were there. You ruined our whole week. Events at the Y are the only thing we can enjoy together, because there's absolutely nothing else for us to do in this town."

Dang. Here's a whole new level of shame. It took me less than a second to pull that alarm. It may take forever for it to stop blaring in my face. So I do what I've been doing. I give him the best apology I can.

"I'm sorry about ruining the game. About everything."

His forehead loses the wrinkles, but he's not finished.

"I don't get to take my wife out very much because it's hard to find fun places with ramps for chairs."

I shake my head. "Yes, sir."

He maneuvers his chair around me and continues down the street. I'm about to head to the house when an idea crosses my mind. I turn around and holler.

"Yo! Sir! Hold up!"

His chair stops and turns back toward me. I jog to meet him.

"Have you ever been to Striker's?"

He frowns more. "You mean that bowling place? Why would I want to go in there?"

"Striker's has awesome ramps for chair bowlers. You can bowl every day. You don't have to wait on a special event to have fun. You should come check it out."

He rubs his chin. "You say they've got ramps?"

I nod. "Sure do. And you won't be the only wheelchair bowler. There are a couple guys who bowl from their chairs every day. And they roll lights out. You should come to Striker's on the Fourth of July. It's going to be a ton of fun. Wouldn't you rather be in a game than watching one?"

He grunts at me and wheels down the sidewalk. I feel bad about what I did at the Y, but telling him about Striker's may even it out, especially if he comes. Hopefully I can make it home without another verbal beat-down or worse.

The only good thing about today is I switch from inside chores to outdoors. After lunch I'm sweeping leaves into a pile in our yard when I hear someone walking up on me. I turn quickly. My eyes widen, but I keep my mouth closed.

"Hi, Lamar. You got a minute? I want to talk to you about something."

I hold tight to my rake in case I need to defend myself. Makeda drops her soccer bag on the bottom step. She has a covered plate in one hand and her other hand is on her hip. I glare at the plate and brace for the worst. I've heard about vengeful women hiding grenades, hot grits, even chemicals in everyday things and catching sapheads off guard.

She takes the foil. "I baked you a dozen chocolate chip cookies."

Dang, those cookies look good. I take two. We sit on the steps and she watches me eat. She pulls a letter from the side pouch of her bag.

"I didn't get the job at MVP camp. I got this letter yesterday. Here, you can read it."

I shake my head and put the cookie back. "I don't want to read it. I don't need to feel any worse than I already do."

She presses the envelope against my chest. "Read it."

Dang. I open the envelope flap, remove the letter, and read it aloud.

*Dear Ms. Phillips,*

*It was my pleasure to spend time with you and your family as I search for the right counselors and assistant counselors for this year's MVP camp. There are so many wonderful things that stand out about you and your family that I'm sure I'll be visiting again sometime in the near future. However, I do have a concern about an incident that happened during the basketball game at the YMCA, and that concern became the primary factor in my decision.*

*As an assistant counselor, your job is to show love to your neighbors, not just when they're right, but even more so when they're wrong. I saw an important opportunity, but you chose not to practice that fundamental teaching of MVP camp. I believe you know which incident I speak of and therefore I will not mention it in my letter.*

*I am so confident in your ability to correct your mistake that I have already put your name back in the hat for an assistant counselor position next year. Have a wonderful time at MVP camp next month, and I hope to see you again soon.*

     *Sincerely,*

     *Harriet Worthy*

     *Advisory Committee Member*

*P.S. Tell your grandmother I said thanks for the peanuts.*

I jerk my head toward Makeda.

"I already called her and told her to toss the nuts," she says.

"Good. Okay, I read it. Are you happy now?"

She places the letter back in the envelope and stares at the step below us. "Nope. I'm not happy at all. Ms. Worthy is right. I owe you an apology."

I snap my neck around to look her in the eyes again. "What?"

She puts those big brown eyes on me. "I'm sorry, Lamar. I wasn't a very good friend or girlfriend. But I want to tell you why I felt the way I did."

"Okay, I'm listening."

"I took the whole thing personal. I thought you were pulling the ultimate prank on me by having the sprinklers go off on the most important day of my life. I completely believed it when I saw Sergio there. I've never seen him at these games."

I shake my head. "He was waiting on me. I didn't even know *you* were there until I saw Ms. Worthy."

She plays with her braids and stares at the ground. "From the moment you walked by me and Ms. Worthy at the Y, I hated you for making me believe you had changed. Then I heard all the rumors about you pulling the alarm because you were jealous of Xavier."

"Jealous! I'm not jealous of X. And I didn't mean to hurt you. I didn't know there was a sprinkler system. But jealousy was *definitely* not the reason I pulled the alarm."

I take two more cookies off her plate. "Dang, Makeda. I've made such a mess of things, I'll probably never get it all cleaned up."

She takes a cookie. "I'll help you."

"You can't help me. It's something I have to do on my own. But these cookies are bangin'."

"Thanks. Will you at least tell me what's on your mind?"

I prop the rake on the side of the porch. "Well

first, I've totally messed up X's chances of playing basketball."

"You mean for the summer?"

"No, I mean forever. He's not smart, Makeda. He gets frustrated because he doesn't understand equations and stuff. That game was his opportunity to shine in front of a bunch of scouts, and I took that from him. He won't pass his algebra class, not without a miracle."

Makeda puts the plate of cookies in my lap. She pulls a soccer ball from her bag, stands on the sidewalk, and bounces it off her knee.

"So who's his tutor?"

"He doesn't have one. Tutors cost a lot of money, and Dad can't afford one."

She catches the soccer ball in her hand. "What if I knew a tutor who wasn't so expensive and could teach it to Xavier like a second language?"

I look at her. "I'm listening."

"I'll make a call, but this tutor isn't free. You got any money?"

"Yeah. It's for my Pro Thunder and that stupid fine I have to pay."

Makeda lets the ball fall in the yard and comes back to the steps. "Didn't you enter Bubba's contest? You wrote an essay, didn't you?"

I stare at the grass. "'A man puts cash on the

counter for what he wants.' That sounds so stupid right now."

She sighs. So do I. I can't believe I'm having this conversation. I turn to her.

"Does this tutor live in Coffin?"

She nods. "Yeah. It's my cousin Kenyan. He's home for the summer from college. He's majoring in mathematics. He's really good, but you're probably looking at two hundred bucks for a few sessions."

A cash register *cha-ching*s in my head. "What! I don't have that much extra money. If I give your cousin two hundred bucks, I can't get my ball."

I watch cars drive by. "And then there's Sergio. We were supposed to go to Holiday World after Xavier's game, but I got in trouble. I completely ruined his birthday. I don't think he'll ever talk to me again."

"You should try. He's your best friend. Apologize. He'll understand."

I give her the plate, get up, and grab my rake.

"Listen, Makeda, that MVP stuff about loving your neighbor is cool, but for me and Sergio, the cheese melted off our sandwich. I'm not down with acting like some punk. I mean, I hate what happened, but he's said some terrible things, and

I'm not ready to hear 'I told you so' for the rest of the summer."

She touches my arm and I turn to her. "Lamar, I've heard some really sad things about Sergio. You're not the only person who could use a friend right now."

I rake at one leaf in the yard. "You think you can just bounce in here and solve all my drama?"

She grins. "Yeah. And I was hoping we could make up under the soccer bleachers."

I drop the rake. The thought of sniffing strawberries makes my big toes rise. Now I know the real reason why she's here; I put these luscious lips of love on her one time, and now she wants them again.

She nudges me. "Go ask your dad if you can walk me home."

"Okay. Wait here."

I go inside. Dad's on the couch watching a ball game. I make my way to the mantel and wait for him to look at me. When he does, I smile.

"Hey, Dad, I know I'm on lockdown, but my girlfriend just came by to see me and I wanted to walk her home. Can I? Please? I promise I'll come right back and finish my chores."

Dad gets up and pulls the curtains back. He smiles, waves, and then turns back to me.

"Thirty minutes. That's it. Hurry up."

"Yes, sir. Thanks, Dad."

I take two hundred dollars out of the Bank of Lamar and stuff the money in my pocket with my inhaler.

I rush down the steps to my girl, and we stroll down the street, hand in hand. There's a soccer game going on, and we leave Makeda's bag next to the hole in the chain-link fence as we climb through. Tiptoeing, we sneak to the very end of the bleachers.

I hug and kiss her twice. It feels so good to be with her, but I've got my mind on my money. What I'm about to do is final.

"Here, take this." I give her the money. "Are you sure your cousin can help X?"

"I'm totally positive, Lamar. Kenyan's getting his master's degree in mathematics."

"Xavier can't find out I'm behind this."

"He won't. I promise."

"Makeda, X has to pass this test on Tuesday."

"That gives Kenyan only six days. But he can do it, Lamar. And you don't have to worry about X finding out it was you, because Kenyan won't tell."

"It's not just about keeping this a secret. It's about my two hundred bucks. Your cousin better handle his business, especially since he's getting paid up front."

# Chapter Twenty-four

At noon on Wednesday, Mason gives me the great news.

"This is your last day, Lamar. You've done an excellent job."

He shakes my hand and I smile. "Thanks, Mason."

"Do you shoot hoops?" he asks.

"No, I bowl. Actually, you're talking to the King of Striker's."

Mason head tilts. "Striker's Bowling Paradise? I haven't been in that place since I was in high school. King of Striker's? You must be pretty good."

"I am. Have you ever heard of Bubba Sanders?"

Mason shakes his head. "Can't say I have. Who is he?"

"The baddest bowler on the planet. He's coming to Striker's on the Fourth of July because he's giving away some bowling gear. Striker's is the place to be on the Fourth."

Mason smiles. "Yeah, it sure sounds like it. Listen, I've got to get back to work. I'll see you around, Lamar."

"Okay, bye, Mason."

On my way home, I cut through Striker's parking lot. Holy guacamole, I smell pizza. The aroma hijacks my body and turns it completely around. My nose follows the smell of cheese to the front doors.

Bubba's contest poster is still taped to the glass. I'm not worthy to even look at his picture after the mess I've made. I cover Bubba's face with my hand.

Dad will mow my grass if he catches me inside Striker's. But he didn't say I couldn't *look* in. I crack the door and peek inside.

I can't believe it. The place is rockin' for a Wednesday afternoon. And it's packed. I open the door wider and release a bigger pizza smell into the parking lot with me.

It smells so good, I close my eyes and pretend

I'm inside. I'm so busy whiffing that someone pushes on the door and it clunks me in the head. My eyelids flip open. It's Sergio.

He stays inside the door and holds it cracked open, like Striker's is his house and he can't have any company.

"Why are you standing out here?"

I rub my head and take a step back just in case he decides to come out.

"I, uh, I'm on lockdown."

He holds the door steady. "So, if you're on lockdown, what are you doing outside?"

"I've been working at the Y, to help clean it up. That was my punishment. It's the worst punishment ever, because I see that stupid fire alarm every day."

Sergio looks behind him and back at me. "Worse than not being able to bowl?"

I shake my head. "Nothing is worse than that. And Dad snatched my bowling pass."

Sergio steps outside. "Dude."

I nod my head toward the door. "Sergio, I just wanted to say . . ."

He puts his hand to my face. "Don't say it. I spent the whole day at Holiday World with my dad and his college friend. There's nothing you can say or do to make me feel better."

"Okay." I watch cars pass by and park. "Anything

new going on in Striker's?"

"Same ol' same ol'. I'm sure you heard what happened to me and Tasha."

I shake my head and shrug. Sergio shrugs, too, as if he doesn't know either.

"We broke up. You were right. She used me."

I stuff my hands in my pockets. "What do you mean?"

He squints at me. "Remember the day you came over and we had that blast session on my porch? Well, after you left, I started thinking about how much money I give her. And I never see any of the stuff she says she buys. I decided to follow her. And I took my camera."

A chill runs through me. "Holy guacamole, what happened?"

Sergio stuffs his hands in his pockets. "She asked for twenty dollars to buy a pair of earrings. I gave it to her and then trailed her to the mall. I got one picture of her and some other dude going to the movies. I got another picture of her buying him a burger, and the worst is one picture of her mixing spit with him. I deleted that one."

"Dang. Are you okay, bro?"

"She didn't visit one earring store. Not one. I trusted her, bro. I'm a saphead."

I kick a pebble on the asphalt. "I'm a bigger saphead than you. I was right about Tasha, but you were right about Billy. You think your rep is shot? This whole town hates me."

We stand side by side, two misused and abused dudes who got chumped to the hundredth power.

Sergio lets out a big sigh. "I got an email from Bubba's secretary. They got my essay."

"Did you win?"

"All it said was 'Thank you for entering, blah, blah, blah, and good luck.'"

"Well, at least you got something. That's kind of cool."

"Yeah, I guess. You should have written one."

I don't answer. If he starts that I-told-you-so stuff, I'm leaving.

Sergio shifts his weight and crosses his arms. "I heard Billy got six months in boot camp."

I nod. "Yeah, that's what I heard, too."

He spits and wipes his mouth. "I'm glad he's gone. He ruined our friendship."

I cut my eyes to him. "What do you mean? Aren't we friends anymore?"

He shrugs. "You dropped me first, Lamar. Then you left me hangin' on my birthday. I'd say our friendship is busted, wouldn't you?"

"I'm going to make it up to you, Sergio. I know you don't think I can, but I will."

"Why? Because Billy's locked up and you don't have any friends now?"

I shrug. "It's way more than that. I'm thinking about going to talk to him. I need to get some things off me."

He throws his hands in the air. "Geez, Lamar, haven't you had enough?"

I stare at the asphalt. "I've had more than enough."

Sergio stares at the side of my face. I can feel his stare. His hand touches my shoulder.

"Dang, bro, I didn't know it was like that. Is Makeda talking to you, or has the cheese melted off that sandwich, too?"

"She came over yesterday and we talked for a long time. She's going to help me figure out some things."

"I was wrong about her, Lamar. My bad, bro."

I crack a grin. "Did you just call me 'bro' twice?"

Sergio rolls his eyes. "Totally slipped."

"Anyway, I'm starving and I've got an afternoon of chores to do. Check you later."

When he opens the door, the sounds of everything I love fill my ears. I can't wait to get back in there.

On my way home, I make one more stop. This shouldn't take long. Billy is on me and I've got to find out where he is. Before I left home this morning, I checked the phone book and got his home address.

I shuffle up the porch steps and knock on the door. It opens and a lady wearing an apron pushes the screen open. She's holding a feather duster just like Mom's. Mr. Jenks must have a cleaning service to help him keep things in order. I smile.

"Is Mr. Jenks home?"

She shakes her head. "No, not at the moment. Can I help you?"

I shake my head, too. "No, ma'am. I need to talk with him about his son Billy."

She shrugs. "Well, I'm Billy's mother. What is it you need?"

Oh, Mylanta. Goose bumps ripple across my skin.

"Do you mean you're his stepmother or something?"

She frowns. "Stepmother? What's this about?"

I get the willies. "I'm sorry. It's just that Billy told me you were dead."

Her face smoothes out. "I see. Yeah, that sounds like something Billy would say. Would you like to come in?"

Heck no.

"No, ma'am. I plan to visit Billy, but I don't know the name of the boot camp."

"You want to visit Billy? I can't imagine why. He's in LaPorte, at Camp Turnaround. It's a good three-hour drive from here."

"What's the quickest way to get there?"

She shrugs. "I don't know. Never been and have no intention of going."

"Oh. Dang. Okay. Thanks, Mrs. Jenks. Uh, glad you're not dead."

She chuckles and waves. "Me, too!"

I walk home and wonder why she never asked my name. She didn't seem to care about Billy at all. Maybe he didn't lie. Maybe she is dead to him.

As I climb the steps to my porch, I hear the television. Dad is watching a Cubs game. He looks at his watch. "It's twelve forty-five, Lamar. Where have you been?"

I tell him and he listens, then lets out a long sigh.

"That's a long trip down I-65, son, almost to Chicago."

I get up to leave. Dad grabs my arm and smiles. "That's why we'll need to leave early. I'll request Saturday off so you and I can take a little road trip. How does that sound?"

"It sounds perfect. I'll be ready."

Dad nudges me. "Guess what? Your brother has a tutor and he promises to help X pass his final exam next week. He's some kind of math guru. Isn't that awesome news? Xavier! Come out here a minute."

My brother appears from his room.

Dad points at me. "Tell your brother the awesome news."

Xavier nods. "Yeah, so this dude walks up and says Coach sent him to me, you know, to help with this algebra. His name is Kenyan and he goes to I.U. He said he gets college credit for helping high school students over the summer and he asked if I would help him. Can you believe that? He asked *me* to help *him*! And *he's* helping *me*! It was crazy, sitting at the table, listening to him. Then suddenly—*bam!*—algebra blew up in my head! I understand it, fool! And he's going to come every day until my test. I knew Coach would come through for me."

Dad chimes in. "And I think taking your medicine every day is helping, too."

X nods. "I forgot I was supposed to eat before taking it. That put the brakes on my stomach drama. And now that I take it at night, it doesn't matter that it makes me sleepy because sleep is what I was going to do anyway."

I turn to Dad. This is the first time my father has smiled since the alarm thing. Seeing his face light up is worth ten times what I paid Kenyan. I hold out a fist to my brother. "Congratulations, X. That *is* awesome news."

# Chapter Twenty-five

Saturday morning, after Dad and I have a monster breakfast, I make sandwiches and pack them away in a brown bag with chips and Gatorade. I rush to my room and stuff everything I'll need in my backpack. I hear his keys jingle.

"You ready, Lamar?"

"Yes, sir, and I made us lunch."

"Got your inhaler?"

I roll my eyes and sigh. "Yes, Dad."

He tells Xavier we'll be back later and to work hard during his tutoring session today. Once we're in the car, it's not long before we're on the freeway. Dad takes an exit for I-65.

"It's a straight shot from here," he says.

I settle in the backseat and unzip my backpack. I take out a brand-new notebook full of empty sheets and my favorite pencil. It's time to get busy on this essay for Bubba.

*Dear Bubba,*

*I should be the winner of a Pro Thunder because . . .*

No, that's dorky. Let me start over.

*Dear Bubba,*

*This is your number-one fan, Lamar, and . . .*

*And . . .* I'm an idiot.

It's too hard. Sergio's right. It will take me two years to write one paragraph. I look up and lock eyes with Dad through the rearview mirror.

"What are you doing?"

"I decided to enter the essay contest."

"Bubba's contest?"

"Yes, sir."

"I thought the deadline had passed on that."

"It's Monday at midnight. But I'm having major trouble getting started."

"Let me hear what you've got so far."

"Okay. 'Dear Bubba.'"

It takes Dad a minute, but he gets a clue. "That's it?"

"Yes, sir."

"Lamar, that sounds like the beginning of a letter, not an essay. You start an essay with your reasons for writing one. For instance, yours should start off with something similar to 'I should be the winner of your essay contest because' blah, blah, blah."

"Yeah, that's right, I forgot."

I try again, but it just won't come. Other than the fact that I think I'm Bubba's number-one fan, I've got nothing. It doesn't matter how long I hold this pencil, the eraser isn't big enough to remove what I've done to Bubba. I close my notebook.

Even though he doesn't know it, I've totally disgraced Bubba by rolling gutters, trusting someone else's advice, and dissing his essay contest to my friends. It's not that I can't write an essay; my problem is it's so dang hard asking for something I *know* I don't deserve.

If I were going to write one, I'd write about how this is the absolute, hands-down, no-questions-asked worst summer of my entire life. I could go on and on about dumb mistakes and even outline them.

All this thinking makes me so tired that I lie across the seat and go to sleep. I'm in a deep dream about me and Makeda when I feel the car slow down. Dad makes a sharp turn and I fall off the seat.

"Are you okay back there?" he asks.

"Yes, sir. Are we there yet?"

"I'm pulling in right now. This place is huge."

The big parking lot is almost empty. Visiting hours start in a few minutes. There are a few people standing at the front door of a huge one-story building at the front of the parking lot. Far behind the building are six long tents. In front of each tent is a line of boys standing in single file. Billy's in there somewhere. I feel it.

Dad gets out of the car. "We have to go into this building and sign in. I hope you brought some form of ID with you, Lamar."

I get out of the car. "I've got my school ID. But Dad, I was hoping you'd let me do this by myself."

He seems surprised. "No problem. I can listen to the radio. You made some sandwiches, didn't you?"

"They're in that bag on the passenger seat. This won't take me very long. I'll be back in no time."

Dad leans against the car. "Take your time, son. I didn't bring you all the way up here to rush. I'm proud of you, Lamar. I really am. Now go get in line."

There are seven people ahead of me. When the

guard opens the door, we form one line. I hear a commotion toward the front. Some lady is arguing with a guard.

"There's nothing in these cookies but sugar, flour, and butter."

"I'm sorry, ma'am. Either take the cookies to your car and go to the back of the line, or I'll throw them in that big trash barrel in the corner. It's your choice."

The lady in front of me turns around and whispers, "I learned my lesson with cupcakes. There was a long line that day and it was so hot outside. I couldn't go to the back of the line and wait again, so that guard tossed all of them in the trash, right in front of me."

I make it to the front of the line. The guard seems a lot bigger.

"Empty your pockets," he says.

I take my ID out and . . . oh no. I've got Billy's cell phone.

"Either take your cell phone to the car or I'll throw it in the big trash barrel."

He looks over the long line of people and begins to shout. "If you have anything other than your ID and five dollars on you, take it back to the car and go to the end of the line or I'll dump it in that big trash barrel in the corner."

He looks back at me. "So what's it going to be?"

I shrug. "Toss it."

He doesn't hesitate, then points over his shoulder with his thumb. "Proceed through the open door and wait for the next guard's instructions."

I take my time moving forward and stare at that door like it's the gateway to hell. As I step through to the other side, a strong odor slaps my face and makes my eyes water. A few people are already seated at tables. They're staring at me.

A uniformed guard wearing a cowboy hat gives me a hard look. He checks his clipboard.

"Name."

"Lamar Washington."

"Visiting."

"Billy Jenks."

He checks off something on his clipboard before glaring at me.

"Do not touch William Jenks or any other resident. Please keep your hands on the table and refrain from any inappropriate conversations or vulgar language. Go to table four."

"Yes, sir."

I inch toward table four. On the ceiling, several brown water stains line up with dark spots on the carpet directly below them. Two short vending machines are the only things in this room besides the chairs and tables. One machine has sodas and the other has chips and candy.

There are twelve card tables in this room. Each one seems far enough away from the others for people to have a private conversation. I don't think I want to hear the conversations in this place.

I put my hands on the table and look around. Tables one, two, five, seven, eight, nine, and eleven have women sitting at them. I bet those are mothers.

If Mom had to visit me here, I'd be so embarrassed and ashamed.

Moments later, the guard with the clipboard turns on a walkie-talkie. In a booming voice, he speaks into the radio and closes the one open door.

"All clear. Bring in the residents."

The room is dead quiet. I'm scared to move. My eyes search for some sign of Billy.

*Click!*

A side entrance opens and a line of guys in white jumpsuits marches in. Some look very young, maybe ten or eleven. Others look as old as Xavier.

In a firm drill-sergeant voice, the guard calls names and table numbers.

"Rodriguez, table two. Masterson, table eleven. Jenks, table four. Jackson, table eight."

They march quickly to their assigned tables with their hands to their sides and eyes straight ahead. Billy's face turns as white as his jumpsuit as he gets closer to me. He stops in front of the chair that has a sign on the back that reads FOR RESIDENTS ONLY.

I whisper. "Hey, Billy."

"No talking!" yells the guard.

"Oh. My bad."

After the last name is called, the guard shouts again. "Residents, be seated! You have exactly thirty minutes, beginning now."

Some of the women immediately walk to the vending machine and get snacks. I don't budge. Billy cuts his blue eyes to me. I stare right back and talk about his momma.

"Why didn't you tell me you knew how to do séances? I would have asked you to bring my mom back from the dead, too."

He slumps in his chair and crosses his arms. "Why are you here?"

"I want to know why you lied to me, Billy. I want to know why you left me out there at the Y when you promised you'd be my lookout guy."

"I don't owe you anything, Washington, and that includes an explanation. You made crazy money with me. You should be thanking me."

"For what? I'm the biggest saphead in Coffin for trusting you, Billy. I thought we were friends, but you were just using me."

"I don't need any friends. I don't want any. I'm

a businessman, Washington. How many times do I have to tell you that? As a matter of fact, I've already got a new business in the making."

I frown. "What?"

"I met two guys in here who have a hookup to brand-name designer clothes and athletic shoes. I'm considering a clothing business. Maybe I'll sell my stuff at Striker's on the weekends. You down?"

"You mean stolen stuff?"

He leans in. "Keep your voice down. What are you trying to do, get me busted?"

I lean in, too. "News flash—you're already busted, Billy. And it doesn't seem like it makes any difference. Didn't you learn anything?"

He leans back in his chair. "Yeah, I learned to stay away from weak chumps like you. I can't believe you rolled all the way here to ask me some punk questions. Why don't you man up, Washington?"

"I'm more man than you'll ever be. While you're touring boot camps around the country, I'll be handling my business like a real man. Bank that!"

I'm wheezing. Dang. I try to cough it out. Something's triggering my asthma. Maybe it's that smell. I cough again and sniffle. Billy stares at me.

"I want my phone back. Where is it?"

I shrug. "Check the trash."

"You owe me for the phone, Washington."

"Take it out of my last paycheck."

"We had something, but you turned out to be a lot different than I thought."

"Yeah, I am. I thought I wanted to be like you, Billy. But you use people."

"I don't use people; I just don't do anything for free."

"There's nothing wrong with doing stuff for free. You should try it."

"That's why you'll always be broke, Washington."

"But I'm not locked up, and I might get to see Bubba on Friday. You won't, because I don't think he makes boot-camp visits. And I can bump my gums when I want, where I want, and for as long as I want. And I don't have to wear a busted white prison jumpsuit every day."

Billy shrugs. "Whatever. Did you bring any money? Dude, I'm dying for a Coke. This is the only time I can have one."

My wheezing comes back stronger. I cough again and stand.

"No, I'm broke, remember?"

I rush to the guard. "Something's making me wheeze in here."

He takes no pity on me. "Then leave. Nobody's making you stay."

I walk by table four. Billy eyeballs me. Just before I get to the door, a whistle blows.

"Time's up!"

Nine guys in white jumpsuits bounce to their feet with their hands to their sides.

"Visitors stay seated until the residents have vacated the visitors' area."

As I listen to the guard bark out names and watch the guys respond by rushing to get in line, I know that my road will never lead here. The guard at the door slips sunglasses over his eyes, then looks down at me.

"I hear you wheezing over here. Get your butt off my property and handle that noise."

"Yes, sir."

By the time I get to Dad, I'm gasping for air. I open the car door and he freaks.

"Where's your inhaler?"

"I left it on the backseat."

He starts the car and turns the air to arctic blast, then snatches the inhaler from the backseat before rushing around to help me get in. I grab the inhaler and prop it in my mouth. I'm so weak. Dad notices and squeezes the medicine for me.

"Relax, Lamar, breathe in, breathe out. Just relax, son. I'll get us out of here."

Dad burns rubber out of the parking lot. "I'll take you to the hospital."

"No, Dad, don't. The cool air is helping me. My inhaler is working."

"You scared me. What happened?"

I shrug. "I think I'm allergic to boot camp."

"Did you see Billy? Did you get your answers?"

I turn to him. "All I want to do is bowl, Dad. That's the difference between me and him. It's about having fun with my friends. Once I figured that out, I had the answer I needed."

I climb over the seat and open my notebook.

"You're going to work on your essay?" asks Dad.

"No, sir. I need to write a letter. But before I do, I need to give you something."

I take two hundred bucks out of my backpack and drop it on the passenger seat.

"This is for my fine."

Dad's eyes widen as he looks from the money to the road to me through the rearview mirror. "Where did you get that kind of money?"

"Hustling with Billy. I was saving for something else, but I need to handle my business first. My fine is my business, not yours, and you shouldn't have to pay it."

Dad pulls over and puts the money in his wallet. "No more hustling, Lamar."

"Don't worry. I won't."

"I'm so proud of you."

I lift my pen and press it to the paper. I'm not writing an essay. What I'm writing is much harder—harder than any essay I've ever written.

# Chapter Twenty-six

**M**onday is the deadline for essays to be postmarked and mailed. It took me all evening Saturday, all day Sunday, and some of today, but I got my letter written. I read it aloud once more before mailing it.

> *Dear Bubba,*
> *My name is Lamar Washington. I'm thir-teen years old and way pumped about you coming to Coffin, Indiana. You are the bad-dest bowler in the universe. I've read your book six times because I love to bowl and I want to be just like you.*

*Unfortunately, I'm not entering your essay contest because I don't deserve to win anything right now. I bowled for money and scammed people doing it. I even rolled two gutter balls on purpose just to make bowlers think I wasn't very good so I could take their money. I've made some really bad decisions and said some bad things. I disgraced you, my idol, and I disgraced bowling, my game. I did other stuff, too, but I'm too embarrassed to talk about it.*

*I want you to know I've changed. I no longer bowl for money and I stay out of the gutter. I'm really sorry and I sure hope you can forgive me.*

*From your number-one fan,*
*Lamar Andrew Washington*

When I drop the envelope in the mailbox, my shoulders lower, I sigh, and there's no doubt in my mind I've done the right thing. I sure hope he accepts my apology.

After doing my chores, I sit at my desk in my room and pull up Bubba's website. His Pro Thunder Giveaway Tour schedule is up, and Coffin is on it. If I don't get off punishment soon, I'll miss Bubba. I'm thinking Dad will take us off lockdown on the Fourth, especially since it's Independence Day.

But now I'm bored to death. There's nothing to do. I hear Xavier vacuuming in the living room. I'm sick of watching television. I'm even sick of surfing the net.

I stretch out across my bed. My ceiling represents me well: blank. I've got nothing going on and it's my fault. I might as well go to sleep.

I don't wake up until nine o'clock Tuesday morning. My life is terrible! I'm up just in time to start my outdoor chores again. I get dressed, eat breakfast, go outside, and freak. Dad has stacked five bags of mulch near the porch steps. There's a note on the top bag.

*Lamar, put this mulch around the trees and in your mother's flower bed. I want it all done today. Dad*

If I ever find the drama fairy who sprinkled all this drama dust in my life, I'll personally pluck her wings. This will take me all day. I can't believe it. I have to spend one whole day of my summer break spreading tree bark chips mixed with cow manure around the yard. Then I have to watch people walk by and sneer at me as if I'm the one smelling like that.

I drop my bandana from my head to around my nose and mouth. I've got my sunglasses on, so maybe, just maybe, no one will recognize me. I opted for shorts and a T-shirt because I don't want that stuff on the bottoms of my jeans. Since Dad made me do this, I borrow a pair of his work boots. I figure it's only fair.

The only exciting thing about today is Xavier took his algebra test this morning and his teacher said he'd post the results by five o'clock online. If X didn't pass his test, I want my money back from Kenyan.

At three thirty, a guy strolls up the sidewalk with a laptop case in his hand. He grimaces. I stop shoveling mulch and stare.

He squeezes his nose. "Is that you?"

I pull my bandana down. "No. It's the mulch."

He chuckles. "I know. I was just playing with you. I'm Kenyan. I know you're Lamar by the way my cousin Makeda described you. Well, your brother finds out today."

I shrug. "I know. Hope he passes."

"Me, too," says Kenyan. "I'll let you know."

I rip open another bag of mulch. Two more bags and I'll be finished. I don't know which smell is worse; this or boot camp. At least this one doesn't make me wheeze.

Soon Dad comes home with pizzas, hot wings, sodas, and chips.

"Come and join us as soon as you can, Lamar," he says with a wink.

I even out a mound of mulch in Mom's garden and wipe my brow.

"Yes, sir."

An hour later, there's so much noise inside they don't hear me come in. Dad screams at the replay of a mammoth home run hit by the Cubs' catcher. Kenyan's laptop has a wireless connection. He keeps checking to see if the grades are posted while asking Xavier about his test questions.

X is really into it. He's got Mom's pink feather duster in his hand and a whisk broom in his back pocket. He points the duster at Kenyan.

"Yo, check it out, K. I talked myself through each one, like you showed me. My teacher tried to hate. He said I was disrupting the test session with my mumbling. I said, 'Whatever,' picked up my desk, and moved away from everybody just so he'd chill. I bet I didn't use my eraser more than twice. I'm the real deal, playa. I own algebra."

Dad bought enough munchies to feed twenty people. Four pizza boxes stacked on one side of the coffee table leave little room for all the chips, hot wings, sodas, and cookies. I sure hope X has passed that test, because Dad went all out.

I walk in front of the television and pull my bandana off my mouth. "Hey, everybody."

Dad and Kenyan hold their noses. X frowns and points at my feet.

"You better not get any of that mulch on my clean carpet!"

I go back to the door and take the boots off.

"I'm just going to get a plate of munchies and sit outside," I say.

No one answers. X eyeballs me as I gather pizza, chips, and hot wings on my plate. He mumbles to me.

"In your face, sucker. I know I aced that test."

"I hope you did," I say, and leave.

The window is open. I hear all the talk and laughs coming from inside. It gets quiet, and more laughter escapes through the window. Then I hear:

"*Wooooo-hooooo!* Yeah, baby!"

The front door opens. It's Kenyan.

I move down the steps and throw my paper plate in our big silver trash can. Kenyan is standing at the base of the steps when I turn around.

"He passed. Your brother got a B-plus. Missed an A by two points."

"What?"

"Yeah, he did it!"

I shake his hand. "Thanks, Kenyan. Thanks a lot for helping X. I really mean it."

He nods. "You're the big man, Lamar. I don't think I would ever do anything like this for my brother." He reaches into his pocket and gives me a piece of paper.

"Here's my cell phone number. Let me know if you need my services again. Next time I'll give you a discount."

I turn away from him to finish my work and see X standing in the window, staring at us. I spin back to Kenyan.

"Did you tell him?"

Kenyan glances up to the window, then back at me. "I swear I didn't."

I freak. "He saw us."

"He should be happy he's got a brother like you."

I glance at the window again. X is gone.

"You don't understand, Kenyan. He hates me."

Kenyan pats my shoulder. "He'll cool off. Don't lose that paper, okay? Take it easy."

"Yeah, you, too."

After I finish the yard, I put away the yard tools and go inside. Dad is still all smiles.

"Did you hear the news, Lamar? Your brother passed algebra."

I cut my eyes to Xavier. "Kenyan told me."

Dad keeps talking. "That is the best news I've heard in a long time. And I think in honor of this day, as of tomorrow you're both off lockdown. Lamar, you can't have your bowling pass back yet, and X, you can't have your ball, but you can go hang out with your friends again. I still need to see a little more from both of you before I give those precious things back."

"Thanks, Dad," I say.

"Yeah, thanks a lot, Dad," says X.

Dad heads for his room. "And with that, I'm going to take a nap before I have to be at work tonight."

X stares at me like those scary dogs that don't bark or wag their tail; the ones that make you uneasy because you don't know if they've got a "licker license" or a "license to kill." A shiver goes through me.

"Why were you talking to Kenyan?"

I shrug. "I just told him good job, that's all."

"I saw him give you a piece of paper. What was on it?"

"Nothing. His phone number, I think. He said if I knew anyone who might need his services, to give him a call. Here, you can have it."

I take the paper out of my pocket and stretch it out to X, but he won't take it.

"You're a terrible liar, Lamar. I heard the whole conversation."

I back up and hope he doesn't walk forward. When I feel the knob of my bedroom door, I turn it, walk in, and lock the door behind me. Maybe I should crawl out my window and run down the street.

Instead, I settle in for the night. Maybe if I'm out of sight, I'll be out of mind, too. But I can only do that for so long. Eventually he's going to come after me.

## Chapter Twenty-seven

I'm up before X. After chores and breathing exercises, I bounce. Even though my yard smells like cow patties, it's a beautiful day in the neighborhood. I strut down the street with purpose. There it is! I push the door open to Striker's. Oh Mylanta! I'm home!

The wonderful cheesy smell of pizza welcomes me back. I've missed this place like crazy. I check to be sure there are still forty lanes. I scan the carpet. Same stains, same colors, everything looks the same, except now I'm here to have fun again, not to make money. I spot Sergio sitting alone at his usual table. He sees me and shouts.

"Dude, you're off lockdown?"

"Yeah! I'll be there in a minute."

I buy two Cokes and take them to his table.

"It's about time you got off punishment, Lamar."

"I know. Here, I bought you a Coke."

"Sweet."

I tell Sergio about my visit to see Billy and how the boot camp guard threw Billy's phone in the trash.

Sergio grins. "That cell was a ball and chain, bro. You couldn't go anywhere without Billy blowing up the phone, making you meet him somewhere to hustle. I'm glad you tossed it."

"Dude, it's a new day. I'm done with Billy."

Sergio grins. "Are we rolling?"

"Is water wet? Dad still has my pass, but I've got a few dollars. Did you get a lane?"

Sergio shows me his waiting-list pager. "When are you buying your Pro Thunder?"

"I'm not. I used the cash for something else."

"I hope it was worth it."

"I got a tutor for X so he'd pass algebra."

Sergio gives me props. "That's tight, bro. That's what's up."

"Plus I had to pay a fine for that Y thing."

"Too bad you didn't enter Bubba's contest. At least you'd have a chance."

I'm not telling Sergio about my letter to Bubba.

That's private. "Yeah, I know. And worse, I'm broke and pathetic again."

Sergio looks around, "You're talking to a dude who followed his ex-girlfriend to the mall and got his face cracked. That's pathetic. I'm just not . . ."

His eyes fix on something over my shoulder. I'm scared to look.

"Dude, what's wrong? Is something crawling on me? What are you staring at?"

He doesn't answer. I peek over my shoulder. Holy guacamole!

A señorita made of the hottest salsa walks toward us. Long, black hair blows off her shoulders like one of those sexy models in a magazine. Her dark eyebrows and darker eyes have me hypnotized until I hear my boy whisper.

"Dang."

She's wearing one of those half shirts that show midsection skin. Sergio's talking to himself. I snap my finger at him.

"Yo, Sergio, who's that?"

He shrugs but keeps his eyes on her. "I don't know, but she's fine with jalapeño cheese."

This Hispanic honey half grins at Sergio and sashays by. He's stuck in stupid. I lean toward the aisle, and Sergio looks over his shoulder so we can rate this beauty from the back.

Wait.

I've seen that butt before. When Sergio turns to me, the fear in his face seems real and funny at the same time as he pleads.

"No way, bro. That can't be."

I break the news. "There's only one girl with a butt so high it looks like someone installed hydraulics in it."

Sergio leans in. "Esmeralda Sanchez."

Word around school claims Esmeralda's butt is wider than the sun and the backs of her legs have never felt the warmth of a summer day.

Sergio scratches his head. "She used to part her hair down the middle and sport two fat braids, didn't she? What's going on? Is everybody changing around here?"

I catch him sneaking another look Esmeralda's way, so I call him out. "What are you going to do about it?"

"Nothing. It's Esmeralda Sanchez."

"Dude, if I had passed on Makeda, I would have lost out on a really awesome girl."

"You're right about that, bro. Makeda is a good catch."

I look up and my best friend winks at me. I nod and take a long chug of Coke. Once again, I lean into the aisle for a look down the carpet.

"Okay, Romeo, she's settled in. Time to bust a move."

Sergio grimaces. "What are you, crazy?"

Flashes of a few weeks ago swarm my brain, and I repeat exactly what I remember him saying to me.

"Go talk to her. I double dare you, with cheese."

He eyeballs me. "Do you know what this will do to my reputation?"

"After Tasha, your rep is invisible. Esmeralda is fine, fool."

Sergio and I look her way again. She's sitting at a table all alone. I can tell he's thinking about it, tapping his fingers on the table and slurping the last of his beverage.

He pushes back in his chair. "Wish me luck, bro."

I hold out my fist. "Luck is for chumps. Handle your business."

Sergio shuffles down the main aisle. I watch him motion to the seat across from her and sit down. It takes me back to when I first took that chance with Makeda. I wonder if he's nervous. Girls usually come to *him*. This is a new thing for Sergio.

The disc lights up. Our lane is ready. I hate to interrupt him getting his mac on, but I'm here to roll the rock. I finally get his attention and hold up the blinking disc. He jogs to me.

"Go ahead and take the lane. I'm going to be a

minute," he says with a smile.

I rent my shoes and grab a ball. On my way to my lane, I hear an announcement over the PA. "Just a reminder that reigning PBA champion Bubba Sanders will be right here at Striker's this Friday at six o'clock to help us celebrate the Fourth of July. Bubba's giving away four of his signature Pro Thunders to four lucky winners. Join us on Independence Day at Striker's Bowling Paradise, where we have tons of fun, all under one roof."

I'll be here. That's for sure. I tune out the people around me and zone in on my game. Those ten white pins remind me of Billy and the other boot campers in their prison gear. Billy's gone for six months. I can't imagine six months without bowling. As the music blares, I pick up my ball. I don't care what anybody says, there's nothing better than rolling the rock.

*POW!*

## Chapter Twenty-eight

**B**y seven o'clock Thursday morning, I'm dressed, finished with my chores, and on my way out of the house with the trash bags when I hear a door open and slam. I know it's not Dad. He's not home from work yet. I turn to see X stumbling toward me, still half asleep, wiping slobber from the side of his face.

"You're just the person I'm looking for. Where are you going? Get back here! I need to talk to you."

I'm taking the stairs two at a time with this Hefty bag over my shoulder like I'm some ghetto

Santa when I hear Xavier's bare feet flap on the porch.

"You've got to come home, Lamar. And I'll be here waiting on you."

I drop the trash at the curb and run down the street. When I begin to wheeze, I pump my brakes and check behind me. He's not there. Striker's doesn't open for another hour, so I pass it and step through the hole in the chain-link fence at the soccer fields.

I make it to the end of the bleachers before taking a puff from my inhaler. As the medicine creeps to my lungs, I slide my back down a wooden post as my face floods with tears.

I've failed at doing things wrong and now I've failed at trying to make things right. I grab my head and say what's on my mind.

"I'm such a loser."

X still hates me. He's going to kill me, I just know it. It's been two weeks since my monumental screwup and I still get dirty looks from people. I don't think they'll ever forgive me. This is the absolute worst summer ever. I need a new plan. Maybe I'll just take a nap, right here under the bleachers, and a really good idea will come while I sleep. Because X is right. At some point I have to go home. But I can't get into trouble again. I'm allergic to boot camp.

I wipe my face and get up. Since I'm not that far away, I take a walk to Makeda's house. Grandma's on the porch, so I knock on the door. Makeda answers with a smile. I try to look cheery.

"I was in the neighborhood and thought I'd stop by. Are you avoiding me?"

She giggles. "Did you forget that I go to MVP camp this Saturday? I've been studying and packing. But I did hear the good news about X. Kenyan said he got a B-plus!"

I'm trying to smile, but the edges of my mouth keep sliding downward. Don't cry in front of your girl, Lamar.

"He knows, Makeda."

She tilts her head. "Knows what?"

"X figured it out. Yesterday he caught me talking to Kenyan, and he asked a bunch of questions. I tried to sneak out this morning, but he woke up before I left. He said he'll be there when I decide to come home. He hates me. He's going to rip my face off. I just know it."

She reaches inside and closes the door. "Let's sit on the steps."

I sit with my girl and go through every possible reason why X would be mad with me, including the reason I believe, which is that my brother's an evil alien from the planet Rage.

"You can't roam the streets forever, Lamar. At some point, you've got to go home. I suggest you wait until your dad is there, too. Then make X talk it out with your dad in the room."

"Yeah, you're right. Anyway, I know you're packing, so I'm going to bounce."

I get up and help my girl to her feet. "Are you coming to Striker's tomorrow?"

"Of course! I wrote an essay and I want to see who this Bubba guy is and find out why you like him so much."

My eyebrows jump. "Are you telling me that before this essay thing you'd never heard of Bubba Sanders?"

Makeda shrugs. "Never heard of him. I love to bowl, but I don't watch it on television."

I shake my head. "Unbelievable."

She playfully pushes me. "I'll see you there, okay?"

Grandma's asleep on the porch, so I kiss Makeda on the cheek. She blushes, opens the screen door, and disappears inside her house.

I manage to stay away until six. Dad's car is at the curb. *Yes.* I look up toward the front door and see X peering out the window at me. Something's going down. I can feel it.

Inside, X stands at the mantel in front of my old

spot. He's got that crazy look on his face, and the room reeks with tension.

"Get over here, Lamar."

I don't budge. "I don't want to fight."

"Neither do I, but I will if you don't get over here."

I take a few steps closer. He crosses his arms. "How much did Kenyan charge you?"

I stall, praying Dad will come out of his room soon.

"What are you talking about, X?"

His voice gets louder. "Don't play with me, Lamar! I talked to my coach. He didn't send Kenyan. Now tell me, how much did you pay him?"

"Two hundred."

"Where'd you get that kind of money?"

"I've been saving for new bowling gear."

Dad appears from his room. "What's going on here? Is there a problem?"

X stays locked on me. "Maybe."

Dad takes a step closer. His eyebrows scrunch. "Don't make me ask again."

My brother doesn't seem to care that Dad's in the room. He steps toward me. I close my eyes and brace for a punch, but all I hear is X's voice.

"I can't believe you helped me. After everything I've done to you. I've been trippin' about a bunch of stuff, even about how to repay you. Then, I figured it out. Lamar, you gave me something I wanted, so I'm giving you something you want."

He moves from in front of the mantel. There's a new trophy in the spot where Mom's note used to be. I step closer and read the inscription:

LAMAR WASHINGTON
MVB
MOST VALUABLE BROTHER

I can't move. I can't talk. X takes it down and I look up at him.

"Can I hold it?"

"It's yours, fool," he says.

He hands it to me as he tells me what he did.

"I took my tallest trophy and had the guys at the shop take the gold plate off and put one with your name on it in its place. I made them take off the basketball dude, too."

A big, shiny Olympic wreath now rests where the gold dude used to pose. I run my fingers across my name on the gold plate at the bottom.

"Dang, X. I don't know what to say."

"Don't say anything until you see this."

He reaches behind his trophies and pulls out Mom's note, safe inside a gold picture frame. He sets it back in its original spot.

"I took it out of your room. I'm sorry. For everything."

I nod. "Me, too."

Dad stands between us. We stare at Mom's note in silence, as if we've never seen it before. For the first time, Dad grabs X and me by our shirt sleeves and pulls us to him. With watery eyes he says to us what Mom used to say.

"How lucky am I? Two superstars in one family. Today you honored your father *and* your mother. Brother to brother."

I feel Mom's presence. Or maybe that's what love in a family feels like. Dad disappears into his room but quickly returns with Xavier's basketball. He tosses it to him. X hugs it and twirls it on his finger. Dad opens his wallet and hands me my bowling pass.

Xavier props his ball under his arm and heads to the door. I stuff my pass into my pocket, shoot Dad a peace sign, and follow my brother out. Yeah, baby.

## Chapter Twenty-nine

Friday morning I take the last few bucks out of my Bank of Lamar and stuff them in my pocket. The box is now echo empty. Oh well, it was fun while it lasted. But it's the Fourth of July and I've got plans for it to be a jaw-dropping, light-up-the-sky, boom-boom kind of day for me and my girl.

Bubba's coming and I'm going to be there, front and center. I'm jittery thinking about Bubba standing inside Striker's. My favorite person inside my favorite place. That by itself is a reason to light up the sky with fireworks.

I'm on my way out when Dad steps out of the

kitchen with a sandwich. X sits on the couch watching a replay of the NBA Finals. I glance at my trophy on the mantel.

"Hey, Dad, I'm gone to Striker's. Bubba's coming today, and I want to be close to the door when he comes in. I'll be home late, okay?"

Dad raises an eyebrow. "Don't forget your inhaler. So are you going to watch fireworks or try to make some of your own?"

X snaps around to look at me. "You got a honey? When did that happen?"

I get my strut on and wink. "I'll be back later to give you duds some pointers. But right now, the L-Train's got a passenger to pick up."

Dad and Xavier laugh as I leave. I keep my strut going because it feels right, it feels like old times. Today is going to be the bomb, I just know it.

On my way down the street, I spot Mrs. Ledbetter watering her flowers. She stops what she's doing when I get close. I don't expect her to speak, but Dad would be hot with me if I didn't. So I slow down and throw up a hand.

"Hi, Mrs. Ledbetter."

"Hi to you, Lamar. Did you like the trophy your brother gave you?"

My Jordans screech to a stop.

"How'd you know about that?"

She sets her watering can on the back of her

car and walks closer to her fence.

"I get into your brother's business just like I get into yours. When I saw him coming down the street with that big monster trophy in his hand, I wanted to know where he got it."

Dang. She's all in X's Kool-Aid, too.

"When I asked him about it, he told me how you got that tutor for him. Your momma would be so proud of her boys. Me and Ms. Gibson was just talking about how you turned things around."

"Thank you, Mrs. Ledbetter."

"You're a fine young man, Lamar. Where are you watching those loud fireworks tonight?"

"Maybe at Striker's."

"Well, you be home right after the fireworks show is over, hear me?"

"Yes, ma'am. I will. Happy Fourth of July, Mrs. Ledbetter."

"You, too, baby."

Down the street, Ms. Gibson's head hangs down again. I hear her high-pitched snore. But it's all good. When those fireworks go off tonight, she'll wake up.

I guess there's nothing wrong with having a few extra mommas in the neighborhood.

I'm inside Striker's at eleven and I can't believe the crowd. It's wall-to-wall people and there're still more coming in. It's crazy how bowling balls sound like thunder as they roll down the lanes. It's even crazier to hear lightning strike inside, but that's exactly what it sounds like when that ball crashes into those pins. There's a nasty storm brewing in here, and I can't think of anyplace else I'd rather be!

As I'm checking things out, I notice some sort of bowling challenge going on. All the lanes are involved. Oh, I know this game!

When the automatic pin-setting machine puts the pins on the lane and you have a gold-colored bowling pin in your triangle of ten pins, if you roll a strike, you get free food at the snack bar! Hurry up and buzz, you stupid disc! I love this game!

Moving through the crowd is tough, but I don't care. There's so much to see and hear. Red, white, and blue streamers loop across the ceiling. Old-school music bangs from the speakers. There's even a clown goofing off, making animals out of balloons and giving them to the kids.

Wait. Is that Trina from Dr. Avery's office standing with those kids and the clown? It is! Our eyes meet and we grin at the same time. She points behind her, and I see Dr. Avery standing on the lane, about to roll. His form needs work, but I don't have time to tell him, because I don't want to miss anything. I give her a thumbs-up and get one back before I move on.

Holy crackers and cream cheese! The snack bar has six people working in it and the lines are still ridiculous. Pizza, hot dogs, popcorn—everything I love is selling by the truckload. This is how it should be all the time, and I'm so pumped to see Striker's packed-out, rock-concert crazy! Today, this is where I live, because I'm not leaving until I have to!

Here comes the hottest firecracker in this place, getting her sexy swerve on as she walks toward me. She's all patriotic in her white blouse, red skirt, and blue sandals.

"Well, don't you look like Ms. Fourth of July," I say with a smil.

Makeda blushes. "Thanks. Did you sign up for a lane?"

I show her the disc. "Of course! As soon as this beeps, I'm ready!"

We stand near an empty bowling ball rack and talk like we just met. It feels great having my girl with me. Soon my beeper disc lights up.

On our way to the lane we spot Sergio and Esmeralda.

"Yo, Sergio! I got a lane! Come on!"

They join us in a game of boys against girls. After Sergio and I cream their corn, I kiss Makeda in front of everybody. Sergio turns and kisses Esmeralda.

The four of us check out carnival games and booths outside in the parking lot. We stop at a radio DJ's table and get free T-shirts. I get blue ones for me and my girl, and we put them on. There's so much stuff happening that time gets away from me. Just as we go back inside and get in line at the snack bar, somebody shouts from the door.

"He's here! Bubba's here!"

I turn to Makeda. "Hold on to my hand. I'm going to move closer."

The crowd tightens. I try to squeeze through and accidentally lose my girl in the crowd.

"Makeda!"

I can't hear her. I don't see her.

Maybe if I stand on the snack bar counter, she'll see me. I look for Sergio, too.

Who are all these people? I bet they're Bubba moochers from other towns. They probably entered our contest, too.

From up here, I see a shiny black Escalade Truck outside with big silver rims. The front license tags spell BOWLN. That's got to be Bubba's ride.

The front doors fly wide open and two big dudes wearing sunglasses strut in with Bubba right behind them.

There he is, in the flesh, my absolute,

hands-down, no-questions-asked favorite person in the whole wide world. His fro is perfect. He looks so sharp in his white shirt and baggy jeans. I'm going to start wearing the exact same thing.

Bubba climbs up and stands on a big box. He turns on a wireless microphone.

"What's going on, Coffin, In-di-ana! *Make some noise!*"

Girls scream, guys bark, old people clap and wave. I'm about to pee all over myself. He's here, in Coffin! Bubba looks just like my poster of him in my bedroom. He sounds just like he does on television. I've got to get closer, maybe shake his hand, or even better, get an autograph.

Bubba talks about how long he's bowled and all kinds of stuff I already know about him. When he finishes, he shouts out to the crowd again.

"Now who's ready to *win new gear*?"

People scream again and Bubba holds up a piece of paper.

"The first Pro Thunder is awarded to John Bailey. Is John in the house?"

From the snack bar counter I watch a happy dude work his way through the crowd. Bubba shakes John's hand and has him stand against the wall. He looks back to his paper.

"The second Pro Thunder is awarded to

Jasmine Maloney! Jasmine, come see me!"

Jasmine screams and jumps her way to the front.

"The third Pro Thunder goes to Makeda Phillips! Makeda, walk this way!"

When I see my girl sashay through the crowd, I can't help but bark it out.

*"Woof, woof, woof!* Extrafine honey in the house! You did it, Makeda! Ma-ke-da! You rock, girl!"

I yell to people around me. "That's my girl!" Based on their expressions, I don't think they believe me.

"And the last one goes to Freddie Johnson. Freddie is now ready with his new gear!"

Freddie slaps high fives with every guy he passes on his way to the front. He even gives Bubba one. Bubba laughs and puts the microphone back to his mouth.

"I need one special person to help me bring these new Pro Thunders in from my truck. Someone strong. Anybody out there like that?"

I hop up and down on the snack bar counter. I wave my hands in the air. I scream so loud, people stop screaming and stare at me wide-eyed and openmouthed. Bubba points at me.

"Okay, young blood, I think you want to help more than anyone else. Hop off that counter and let's get busy. While we get the winners their new gear, my staff wants to hand out free Bubba Gumballs. So form a line and get your gum! Come on, young blood, I'm waiting!"

I leap down and push through the crowd. "'Scuse me, coming through. I'm Young Blood."

When I reach the front, he shakes my hand and, over the microphone, asks my name. Before I can answer, I hear Sergio yelling out.

"He's the King of Striker's!"

Bubba's eyes light up. "You roll?"

"Yes, sir, I do. I've got your book and everything. I've read it like six times."

"Really?"

I wink at Makeda and she blows me a kiss on my way out. Bubba's bodyguards stay near the front door as Bubba and I head to his truck. He hands me two bowling bags.

"What's your real name, son?"

"Lamar. I'm your biggest fan, Bubba."

He freezes. "Lamar Washington?"

I wipe imaginary dust off my shoulder. "You've heard of me?"

"I got your letter. It's in my glove compartment."

The edges of my smile droop. I can't believe he got it already. And worse, he read it. But I'm beyond freaked that he's got it with him.

"I'm really sorry, Bubba." I put the bowling bags down. "Do you want me to leave?"

He shakes his head. "I want you to give your-self a break. We all make mistakes, young blood. You'll make a thousand more before you die. As long as you learn from your mistakes, it's all good."

"Thanks, Bubba. Can I talk to you about something else?"

"Since you're my number-one fan, you can talk to me about anything."

"I've got this problem."

Bubba crosses his arms. "Lay it on me."

"My absolute best friend picked me to go with him to Holiday World for his birthday."

Bubba's eyebrows jump. "That place has a wicked roller coaster."

"Yeah, that's what I've heard. Anyway, I got in trouble the night we were supposed to go and left him hangin'. He ended up doing Holiday World with his parents."

"*Oooooh.* How did you make it up to him?"

"I haven't. I was hoping you'd let me bring him out here to meet you."

"What are you waiting for? Go get him!"

I barely hear his last words because I'm scrambling to fight the crowd.

"SERGIO! *SER-GI-O!*"

I don't hear a response. I turn back toward the door and see the microphone Bubba used lying on the front desk. I scramble through the crowd, grab the mike, and turn it on.

"Sergio Reyes, Bubba wants to meet you! Get up here now! Hurry!"

Soon, I hear, "Move please, I'm Sergio, the guy Bubba's looking for. Could you move and let a guy through?"

He pushes his way by the last cluster of Bubba groupies and I grin at him.

"Come on, bro. I want you to meet Bubba."

Sergio's face lights up. "Holy guacamole."

We race out to his truck.

"Bubba, this is my best friend, Sergio Reyes."

Sergio freezes, but I completely understand. Bubba reaches down, takes Sergio's hand, and shakes it.

"Lamar told me you had a birthday not too long ago."

Sergio's smile fades. "It really wasn't that good."

Bubba nods, "Sorry to hear that, young blood. I tried to give something to Lamar for helping me out, but he insisted that you have it."

Part of me wants to push Sergio underneath Bubba's truck and take the gift for myself. But then I see Sergio's face. He's real eager to see what Bubba has for him. He gives me a look that accepts all the apologies I've tried to give him in the last week.

Bubba signals for one of his bodyguards.

"Do we have The Truth in a twelve?"

"I've got one in my trunk," says the bodyguard.

"Bring it to me."

While we wait, Bubba answers every question we've got. He even tells me his secret for keeping his fro nice and round.

"I've got a barber who mixes a secret solution and pours it on my fro once a week."

"It's not fertilizer, is it? My dad puts a secret solution on our grass once a week."

Bubba laughs. "I hope not."

"Here you go, Bubba," says the bodyguard.

Bubba gives Sergio a scruffy gray bowling ball that doesn't shine or have any markings on it. It's ugly, like a house ball, except Bubba's holding it and smiling.

"Happy birthday from Lamar and me. This is a twelve-pound tester of my newest line of bowling gear, called The Truth. It's a one-of-a-kind, because The Truth isn't available to the general public yet. It's not pretty, but I'd really like for you to try it out and let me know how it rolls. Stick your fingers in the holes and see how it feels."

Sergio jams his fingers inside. "Perfect! It's a perfect fit! No way!"

I get as close as I can. "Let me see, Sergio. Can I hold it?"

Bubba taps me on the shoulder. "We've got work to do, Lamar. Four people are still waiting on their Pro Thunders."

"Oh yeah, my bad, Bubba."

Bubba and I head toward Striker's front doors, both of us carrying two bowling bags with heavy stuff in them, while Sergio walks like a zombie beside us with his new gear. Bubba keeps talking.

"Friendship is a Bubba-sized trophy, Lamar. Don't ever take friends for granted."

"Okay. I promise."

Bubba grins. "I'm glad I met you, Lamar, King of Striker's. What's my rule?"

"Stay in school."

"Now that's cool. Thanks for your help."

I strut to deliver his Pro Thunders to the winners. Before he leaves, Bubba shakes my hand again. He honks as he pulls out of the parking lot, and I can't believe what's just happened. Bubba came to Coffin and talked to me. Sergio pushes me on the shoulder and breaks my trance.

"This is the best birthday gift ever. Thanks with cheddar, bro."

Makeda and Esmeralda break through and listen to us relive the greatest five minutes of our lives. Makeda's ball is so new, it doesn't even have finger holes in it. It's all glittery, with red and black swirls in the design.

"I think we should bowl, in honor of Bubba," says Sergio.

I cross my arms to pose. "I totally agree."

Sergio strikes a pose, too. "Did I ever tell you that twelve is my lucky number?"

"Dang, Sergio, aren't you tired of losing?"

I'm waiting for him to say something back, but instead, Sergio's looking over my shoulder again. He can't be checking out a hottie, since Esmeralda and Makeda are with us. So I turn around. It's Mason, the security guard. I stretch out my fist.

"Hey, what's going on?"

Mason bumps my fist and chuckles. "You sure can yell, Lamar. My family is still laughing at you screaming on the counter. When I told them I knew you, they didn't believe me. We've been here all day! Thanks for the idea."

"I told you bowling is the bomb, Mason."

"You sure did. Well, have fun. See you around."

"Yeah, later, Mason."

Sergio nudges me. "Dude, who was that?"

"He's the security guard at the Y. I worked with him. He's cool people."

My disc lights up and I get right in Sergio's face.

"Looks like your good day just came to an end. Our lane is ready."

He doesn't back down. "So the question is, are

*you* ready for your streak to die? Because that's exactly what's going to happen."

I laugh at my friend. "Just to show you I'm not worried, I'm buying the snacks today."

We stroll to the snack bar and order pizza and drinks for the four of us.

Sergio nudges me. "Dude, I really like Ezzi."

"Man, I already know guys are going to be after Makeda when school starts again."

We glance at our superfine honeys. I haven't felt this great in weeks.

Esmeralda and Makeda talk, giggle, and eat pizza while we bowl. It doesn't take long to spank Sergio for the twelfth time. As a matter of fact, I tack on numbers thirteen and fourteen before we head back to the snack bar to order pizza. Once we find a table, I crank up the motor on my mouth.

"Yo, Sergio, check it out. Just because the King of Striker's takes a few days off doesn't mean he's no longer king. I was just taking a royal break."

Sergio fakes a sneeze. "Oh, excuse me. I'm allergic to royal bull. Getting used to this new ball is going to take time."

Two large pizzas later, I pat my belly. Makeda pats hers, too, and giggles. I look over at my boy and he nods at me.

"Thanks, Lamar. That was good and on time."

"Yeah, thanks, Lamar," says Esmeralda.

I give Sergio a high five. "It's getting dark out-side, bro. The really good fireworks are going to start soon. I'm going to walk Makeda to her house so she can drop off her new Pro Thunder. We have a special place to watch the show, so I'll catch you later."

Sergio takes Esmeralda by the hand and winks at me. "We're going to watch the fireworks some-where nice. I'll call you."

Sergio winks at me and I wink back.

On my way out, someone yells. "Hey, kid!"

I scan the lanes and grin when I see who's in lane seventeen. I tell Makeda, "I'll be right back."

I walk into his bowlers' area. He pushes his wheelchair to meet me.

"You were right. My wife and I haven't had this much fun in years. We're thinking about joining a league. Thanks for telling me about it. My name is Charles."

I shake his hand. "I'm Lamar. See you around."

I take my girl's hand and we walk out of Striker's, into the evening air.

"You know that guy, Lamar?" she asks.

"Sure do."

We drop her ball off and then sneak through the hole in the chain-link fence. The first set of fireworks shoots across the sky. The boom rattles inside me. This is what summer is all about; free and easy, hanging with my friends. I put my arm around Makeda. She looks at me.

"There were a lot of people at Striker's today."

I nod. "The word is getting out. Bowling is the baddest game in town."

"Yeah," she says.

My eyebrows rise. "You know what I have a taste for?"

"What?"

I lick my lips. "Strawberries."

She giggles as I lean toward her, and I'm not sure if the fireworks are from our kiss or the glittery sky on this awesome Fourth of July.

# Acknowledgments

I thank God for everything, especially this journey. But no one takes a journey like this one alone. My path prior to publication has been guided by caring professionals in the publishing world, incredible people such as Bernette Ford, Eileen Robinson, Harold Underdown, Dara Sharif, Emma Dryden, Christine Taylor-Butler, Kent L. Brown, Jr., Neal Shusterman, and countless workshop and conference hosts. Critique partners are invaluable, and without the feedback from Diane Bailey, Jenny Bailey, Carrie Garfield, Tim Kane, Juliet White, and Petula Workman, I would have submitted something very different from the story I have. My entire family and host of friends showed support, love, and encouragement as I stepped out into this new adventure. And once I was ready, I was blessed with the absolute, hands-down, no-questions-asked best agent ever, Jen Rofé, who knew my fabulous editor, Kristin Daly Rens, would love this story as much as I do. To all of you, I say thanks so much for walking with me.